A Story You Need to Read

Mitchell Person opened his small construction company in the bad part of town because that was the only place he could afford. He wasn't interested in urban renewal. He wasn't interested in turning his city's social welfare system on end. He only wanted to use his hands and tools to build things of which he could be proud.

But his spirit of self-reliance spills over into the nearby neighborhood, starting a magnificent rebirth of the city's worst slum.

Not everyone appreciates Person's efforts. An ambitious politician and greedy union boss yank Person into a fiery racial controversy that threatens to destroy all he has built. He faces the choice of succuming to their wishes, or sticking by his principles and losing everything.

Share in this story. It will change you.

The Break Room talks about special interests:

The threshold between a worthy cause and an unworthy quest for power is too easily crossed.

...welfare agencies:

She saw the inherent problem with an agency that, in a perfect world, would eventually eliminate the need for itself.

...poverty:

Our country can't afford to keep poor people locked in these neighborhoods. We need strong minds and bodies, driven by their own selfish need to produce, create and chase profits.

(continued)

...government:

> *While our government argues with itself about whether this benefit is a right, or whether that benefit is fair, or whether we need to increase or decrease this benefit, the poor feel more and more helpless.*

...the media:

> *They have relinquished agenda-setting to industry and government. Ironically, news reporting can't be truly objective when the news is purposely and subjectively created by someone else.*

...motivations:

> *Revenge? Power? Control? Greed? Those are not tools for building. Those are weapons of destruction to keep other people from reaching the top.*

...and much, much more!

The Break Room
A Story of Self-Reliance

The Break Room

A Story of Self-Reliance

By Kyle Hannon

Herbert,

It was great talking to you. Continue to be entertaining. Enjoy the book

[signature]

8-23-87

Filibuster Press, Elkhart, Indiana

The Break Room
A Story of Self-Reliance

By Kyle Hannon

Published by:

Filibuster Press
55836 Riverdale Drive
Elkhart, IN 46514-1112

Cover design by Gregory R. Miller, Indianapolis, IN

To Shawn, a wonderful wife,
mother and editor.

Note to the reader:

The characters in *The Break Room* are fictional. They do not represent any actual people living or dead. If they seem similar to you or someone you know it is because they reflect many of the ambitions and motivations in us all. Likewise, none of the associations, governments or policies represent specific organizations or policies. Rather, they represent the types of organizations that can exist and the environment in which their policies and activities thrive. The goal of *The Break Room* is not to indict any actual person, organization or policy, but to provide the reader with an opportunity to explore the kinds of events that can happen within our social and political systems.

"We cannot think of being acceptable to others until we have first proven acceptable to ourselves."

--Malcolm X

"It is difficult to make a man miserable while he feels he is worthy of himself and claims kindred to the great God who made him."

--Abraham Lincoln

ONE

The apartment was trashed.

While working on a fresh cigarette, building superintendent Sam Jefferson surveyed the damage. Draperies had been ripped from their rods and thrown about the place. In the kitchen piles of unwashed dishes had been knocked to the floor and kicked around. Empty beer cans and a broken whiskey bottle lay on the damp carpeting. The walls were polka-dotted with holes made by feet, fists and furniture. Every window was broken and someone had taken the time to leave a pile of human feces in the middle of the main room.

Despite the mess, Jefferson was nonchalant. He had worked at the Brookview Armes housing project long enough to expect tenants to attack their apartments with uncivilized rage whenever they were evicted. Unfortunately, he could not stop it.

Brookview was heavily subsidized by government money, and with the government money came a pile of government regulations. Although Jefferson was in charge of the place, he had little leeway in its operation.

For example, he could evict tenants for a specified list of transgressions ranging from prostitution to drug dealing.

However, unlike in private-sector apartments, the evicted tenants were automatically granted a 10-day grace period to find new housing.

It was rare that his tenants did not spend a larger portion of their 10 days smashing their current apartment rather than looking for a new one. He could do nothing. Once, he called the city housing authority to complain about the damage caused by the "10-day rule." He was referred to the state human services agency which claimed to be merely implementing federal regulations. The federal housing department explained that the policy was in effect to protect underprivileged citizens from being taken advantage of by their landlords and left homeless.

Jefferson shrugged his shoulders, as he did every time he thought about his bureaucratic adventure, and proceeded with the task at hand, which was to board up the windows and lock the door. Eventually, he would have enough units locked and boarded that he could apply to the feds for a renovation grant. In the mean time, Brookview would look more and more run down while fewer and fewer apartments were available to needy people. By the time the renovation grant came through, the clean-up would cost more than if each job had been handled at the time of destruction, due to additional problems caused by setting stains, likely water damage and rodent infestation. It didn't make sense to Jefferson that he do it this way, but Jefferson had learned it was just easier to follow the government procedures.

When he first got the job of building superintendent, he treated the trashed apartments much differently. Initially he tried to hunt down the ex-tenants to make them pay for the damage. He quickly realized that it was almost impossible to locate them and even if he could have found them, they would not have any money to cover costs. More often, he dodged a bullet, blade or fist for his effort.

One time he decided to clean a vandalized apartment himself. He worked on his hands and knees scrubbing floors, patching walls and replacing windows. The government procedure required him to pay for the supplies out-of-pocket and apply for reimbursement. The reimbursement for his work did not come for two months. That was the last apartment Jefferson cleaned.

He resigned himself to letting the system work its course. When his renovation grant came through, he would hire a team of union-wage workers to get the units back in order. Then he would begin sorting through the applications for housing and filling the units with new tenants. And the cycle would begin again.

Such was life in the blighted sections of Washington City.

****

"Why haven't you moved the hell out of here?" The question came from a client who had just hired Mitchell Person to renovate a small dentist office in a nearby suburb.

He continued, "I'm not insulting your shop. I mean, it's great. No, it's beautiful. The craftsmanship that went into restoring this old building is truly remarkable. But every other building around here is a run-down, crime-ridden trash heap. Walking out of here is going to be like going from Paradise Island into shark-infested waters. I'm sure you could find a better neighborhood, so why do you stay here?"

Person pushed paperwork aside with his strong, slender arms. He was slightly taller than average with a sinewy build that implied impressive strength. His muscles were built not from time in a weight room, but from hard manual work and a passion for his own personal productivity.

He stood and looked around his shop while he answered. The once run down factory now shined. Years of grime had been scrubbed away. Broken and lost woodwork had been replaced and refinished. The various saws, routers, drill presses and other tools were neatly arranged in a way that looked efficient to even a casual observer. One need not understand woodworking to appreciate the masterful set-up.

"I did a good job here. I like the way it suits me, so I see no reason to leave," Person said.

The client just shrugged. He was drawn to Person's Fine Woodworking after he saw a room addition Person built for one of the client's friends. The new client knew just enough about construction to recognize supreme craftsmanship. In the end, that mattered much more to him than the fact that Person's shop was in one of the worst neighborhoods in the city.

Person's Fine Woodworking was a relatively new business in town which prided itself in its new way of doing things. At age 27, Person had quit his carpentry job with a large firm to open his own shop. He had been frustrated with the way things were run by his old employers.

Now, he was boss. As he watched his new customer return to his car he reflected on his old job. Just six years ago he had worked for Davis Construction Company, one of the largest, most respected construction companies in the city. Davis Construction owed its success to a close-knit relationship with the Associated Council of Carpenters, known as the ACC. The ACC had started as a fledgling carpenters' union, but had quickly grown to encompass building trades other than woodworking.

Davis Construction was large enough and employed a wide-enough selection of craftsmen to assemble a building from start to finish. They boasted a roster of specialists who could pour a concrete foundation, construct a framework of any material, hang drywall, paint the finished product and accomplish virtually every task in between. Every worker was a dues-paying member of the ACC.

As an employee of Davis, Person was required to join the union. At the time, he was pretty indifferent about unions. They seemed to make sense because without the protection of a strong organization workers would be exploited by the company bosses. On the other hand, he felt that unions sometimes made outrageous demands that a profitable company could not meet. He wasn't sure which viewpoint, if either, was correct so he joined the union, paid his dues, and went to work.

One day he and three other carpenters were leaving the shop to begin work on a new boat house for a wealthy client. Person noticed that their supply truck was loaded with standard, rather than treated, lumber for their project even though they would be building in a high-moisture area.

Person approached the site supervisor -- a fat, grumpy man whose red nose betrayed years of heavy drinking -- and asked why they were not planning to use treated lumber.

"I dunno," he responded.

"Well, don't you think we should suggest a wood upgrade to the client or at least double-check the work order to make sure the loading dock didn't make a mistake and put the wrong wood on our truck? Otherwise, we're going to spend the day building a boat house that will probably rot within five years."

"Listen smartass. You ain't hardly been around here long enough to know what the hell you're talking about. When I want your opinion, I'll ask for it. But don't hold your breath waiting."

With that settled, Person went to work and completed the job. That evening he was sharing a pitcher of beer with some of his company friends and was talking about the day's events.

"Why do you suppose he wouldn't even check the work order to make sure the loading dock didn't make a mistake? Even his lazy behind could have walked fifty yards back to the office to check paperwork."

Person's friend Ray White chuckled at Person the way an adult snickers at a child who asks a naive question. "You don't understand how this place works, Mitch. Fat Simon wasn't promoted to supervisor because of his attention to detail. He's there because of seniority. But let's pretent he cared enough to check your question. What if he found a mistake? Then he would've had to file an error report with the front-office ACC rep. The front-office rep. would have to evaluate the error and decide if Simon would be allowed to direct the loading dock supervisor to correct the error. The loading dock supervisor would have to ask the loading dock crew to remove the wrong lumber and replace it with the right lumber. That all takes time Simon doesn't want to spend."

"I'm not sure I believe you, but even if you're right, wouldn't it be worth it to go through all that effort if it means a better finished product in the long run? I mean, I feel awful having just worked on an expensive project that may not last even five years. That client Mr. Gentry will be furious."

"Don't kid yourself. Gentry has more money than either of us could count. He'll pay his bill, and when the thing falls apart he'll pay us to build another. You're worried about non-treated lumber that might not last five years? We could've built it out of blocks of ice that wouldn't last five hours and Gentry's bill would still get paid. That's the bottom line isn't it?"

Person looked down at his mug. "I always thought the bottom line was to make something you can be proud of."

Ray laughed again. "Maybe if you're building log cabins in the woods, but not here. This is big-time construction, Mitch."

Person glanced up. "I might say something to Mr. Davis. He can't be happy having his name attached to some half-assed project, especially if the problems were caused by some careless loading-dock mistake that could've been corrected in 15 minutes."

The smile vanished from Ray's face. "No. No. No. That's the worst thing you could do. If you try to go around the union procedure they'll cut your balls off. Besides, Ron Davis doesn't care about one little boat house. He's concerned about getting new projects for his company. If you have to talk to somebody, talk to your union rep."

"Thanks, but my union rep is fat Simon."

They both laughed at the irony and refilled their mugs.

The next day Person came into the carpenter's shop early

and headed straight for the secretary's desk. The shop was a small warehouse that stored dozens of virtually every kind of tool imaginable. There were stationary tools for in-house projects, portable tools for on-site work, power tools, hand tools and even a few antiques that had never been discarded. One secretary was assigned to the carpenters' shop to keep track of the flow of tools in and out of the shop. She also shuffled all the paperwork for every contract involving the carpenters' section of Davis Construction.

Within a couple of minutes, Person found the materials list from yesterday's boat house project. There, at the top of the list, was a request for a delivery of *treated* lumber. Person made a quick photocopy, which he pocketed, and returned the original to where he found it.

That afternoon Person left with all the carpenters who were done working for the day. He talked and joked with his colleagues on the way out and drove off. But after driving around the block for a few minutes, when he was sure no other carpenters would be near Davis Company, he turned back and headed toward the main office. Carpenters worked an early shift so he knew the management office would still be open for two hours.

The receptionist in Ron Davis' office was young, blonde and beautiful. Person smiled. "I'm one of Mr. Davis' carpenters and I need to talk to him about a major error in a project we did. It was a project for Mr. Gentry."

She jotted down a few notes, smiled politely, excused herself and entered Davis' office.

After a couple of minutes she returned. "I'm sorry, but Mr. Davis said there are procedures that are to be followed for reporting errors. He suggested you talk to your union rep."

The next morning, Person came into the shop a little later than normal. He didn't smile. He didn't talk to his friends. Instead, he walked right up to fat Simon and handed him a folded piece of paper. Simon opened it to see a copy of the Gentry boat house materials list. Person had circled the request for treated lumber and had written, in three-inch letters, "I Quit!" Person turned to leave.

"Okay Mr. Smartass, where do you think you're going," bellowed Simon, causing all the other carpenters to stop and watch the scene.

"To build log cabins in the woods," replied Person. He winked at Ray White, walked out the door, and that was the last time Mitchell Person was associated with Davis Construction Company or the ACC.

Today Person's expired union card was framed and displayed in his office. To him it served as a reminder of his commitment to do things better. So far, he had.

As a non-union carpenter, he found it very difficult to get contracts. Government projects were completely off-limits. Most large businesses would not award him a bid either. But he managed to win several smaller projects, and now he had enough work to employ four other carpenters in his business, non-union of course.

All told, Person was very pleased with himself and his company. He considered himself one of those entrepreneurs who was building a successful business from the ground up.

That was three years before the protests.

TWO

Ron Davis sorted the paperwork on his desk and smiled to himself. He was satisfied with his business and his life. Setting his papers aside he lifted his heavy but well-dressed frame from his chair and moved to peer from the window overlooking his company.

Like many of his friends in their late forties, Davis was fighting with thirty pounds that he simply couldn't seem to remove from his waistline. Also, he was running out of ways to make his thinning, graying hair look good, but that's what he was paying his hair stylist to worry about. Based on the comments from acquaintances that Davis looked stately, he figured that both his stylist and his tailor were earning their money.

Besides, he already had a motherly wife, three sons and a beautiful daughter, though the daughter troubled him sometimes. His family made a handsome portrait. On top of that, he was getting his great-looking receptionist about once a week. Yes, life was wonderful.

Business was booming like never before. Davis was proud because he made this business what it was. They were winning contracts right out from under the noses of his few remaining competitors. And he, Davis, was responsible. Some critics quietly -- none wanted to cross Ron Davis publicly -- suggested that some means of questionable legality were used to secure many of the government projects and other major contracts awarded to Davis Construction Company. Nothing, of course, could be proved.

Davis had started as an ACC carpenter many years ago. Even though he was now officially management, he loudly boasted that he was still a member of his old union. Most people laughed at this humble-sounding statement, because they knew he was more than just a member. He still called the shots at the union headquarters.

This cooperation between the ACC and Davis Construction was the main reason for Davis' success. Potential customers knew that if they contracted with Davis, their project would not be delayed by labor problems. Mysteriously, some major contracts that were awarded to other companies became profit-consuming hassles because ACC workers went on strike half-way through the job. The strikers always cited unsafe or unfair working conditions as the justification for their walk-out, but observers whispered that the strikes were started by Davis as punishment for not awarding a lucrative contract to his firm. Most construction companies got the message and backed away from direct competition with Davis, and businesses with large contracts to award were less-than-vigorous about pursuing competing bids.

Davis' rise to power was still one of the favorite stories told in the union halls around the state. As an all-state running back in high school, he was popular in his home town. He might have met his ultimate potential in high school, like many of his teammates, had he not stumbled upon the ACC.

After graduation, proud high school alumnus John Bosworth - owner of a large construction firm - offered Davis a job as a carpenter. Davis accepted, though he didn't really enjoy working very hard and wasn't trained as a carpenter. His sloth quickly became apparent to his co-workers who began riding him hard to try to get him to carry his share of the work.

Davis was frustrated and angry at his co-workers. After a couple years, he was thinking about quitting when Charlie Hayes, one of his few friends in the company, invited him over to his house for a beer. He said there were some people he wanted Davis to meet.

When Davis arrived, Hayes introduced him to two tall, strong-looking men with rugged faces that looked as if they had experienced countless conflicts and hard-fought victories. They were from a new labor union, the fledgling Associated Council of Carpenters, and they had been eyeing Bosworth's construction company as a ripe recruiting field. They gave their pitch.

"We have been hearing some complaints about the working conditions at Bosworth," said the first one. "People being pushed too hard and not being paid enough for their effort."

The second chimed in, "And the older guys are always jumping all over the rookies making them do more than their fair share."

"Our union believes in fair working conditions. It's time for the workers to demand what is owed them. It's time for John

Bosworth to stop exploiting the very people who have made him rich."

With those short statements, Davis was hooked. He just stared at the two men as if they were saviors from above. He felt abused at his job and now here was help.

"Have you ever seen Bosworth's house?" continued the first man. "It's a mansion with a beautiful view and a full staff of servants. Does any one of his employees live in a mansion with servants? Of course not, because John Bosworth makes his house payments on the backs of underpaid workers."

Davis and the old high school football team had been invited to Bosworth's home for a "team appreciation cookout," so he knew the house was very nice. Also, he knew the "servants" consisted of a guy who cut the lawn once a week and a maid who cleaned the house five times a month. Neither lived on the premises or depended solely on Bosworth for their living. But Davis liked what he was hearing from the ACC recruiters and did not wish to correct them.

"When is the last time you saw Bosworth hammer even one nail?" asked the second man. "You do all the work. You feel exhausted at the end of the day. Yet you go home to a rented apartment while Bosworth sits on his ass in an air-conditioned office then pampers himself at the end of the day by going home to sit by his swimming pool while a maid serves him cocktails.

"Sure he has a right to make a profit. But there is profit, and there is abuse. Believe me, he can afford to give every one of you a better salary and better benefits and still enjoy a huge profit.

"The ACC's goal is simple. We believe every carpenter

in the state should be treated fairly and should be able to earn a decent living at his trade. We want you to help us carry that message to your fellow workers."

The room was silent while Davis and Hayes looked at the two men and the two men looked at Davis and Hayes. Davis spoke first. "Damn straight."

The ACC reps explained some basic recruiting techniques to the two rookies. They said it was important to keep silent about their efforts because Bosworth would try to break them as soon as he found out what they were up to. The goal was to be strong and solid before he knew what was happening. Therefore, Davis and Hayes would need to choose prospective members carefully, prospects who were disgruntled and who would not talk to supervisors about the ACC. When Davis and Hayes had found ten other men to join, they were to call the ACC reps and receive instructions about the next step.

The next day, Davis reported for work with a new vigor and enthusiasm. His supervisors noticed the change but did not suspect the reason.

Months later Bosworth was in his office when one of his most-trusted supervisors rushed in.

"John, some of the workers are trying to organize with the ACC!"

The ACC was not yet the powerful union it would become in later years, but most construction companies in the state knew about it. A few firms were already unionized. Most were still non-union.

Bosworth had been working out numbers trying to put

together a bid for a major suburban housing development. Business had been slumping slightly and he needed this contract. He was a kindly man with distinguishing grey at his temples. He enjoyed his company's profits because they enabled him to buy nice things and to do favors for people. In his mind these two actions caused people to view him with respect and admiration.

Due to his history of generous donations of both money and man-hours, Bosworth was one of the first community leaders charitable organizations approached when they were planning a new program. He enjoyed his reputation as a person who liked to help others.

Quite frankly, he did not believe his employee who now interrupted his work. Like most business owners, he was certain that he treated his workers fairly, no, generously. Why on Earth would they want to unionize? Didn't they view their boss as a kindly father figure, a pillar of the community?

He set down his pencil and looked at his friend for a moment. When he finally spoke it was with a calm, even voice. "Bob, I do not believe my workers would get involved in union shenanigans. Surely you are over-reacting to something or you are getting bad information."

"I know what you're thinking John. I couldn't believe it either. For the last couple of months I've notice a few of the guys huddling together whispering, and they would always stop talking and look at me whenever I walked within earshot. I overlooked it because the guys who were involved ain't our best workers. They do okay, but they ain't ready to lead a job or nothing like that.

"Last night I was going over to Bart's late to watch some movies he rented and I stopped at The Tanker bar to pick up a six-pack. You know, they have a package liquor store attached to the bar. I rarely go there because it's a big labor hangout and I don't feel comfortable around those guys. Anyway, the store is on one side of the bar and the tavern is on the other, so from the store I got a clear view at everybody in the tavern.

"In one corner about fifteen of our guys are sitting around drinking and listening to one guy who is standing at the table talking about you, saying you are unfair, saying you exploit all your employees and that you live in a huge mansion with live-in servants. The other guys keep cheering him on. Then he starts telling them that the ACC is their salvation and that now is the time to act.

"I listened for a while but I couldn't hear everything clearly and I wanted to get out of there before any of them saw me. What are we going to do?"

Bosworth felt his insides knot up, but outwardly he remained calm. "I believe we must do what we can to defuse them. Perhaps I should meet with their ring-leader and see if I can reason with him somehow. Who is it?"

"Ron Davis."

Bosworth fought to retain his composure, but Bob could see a flash of shock and dismay in his boss' eyes. Of all the employees for whom Bosworth had done favors, Davis owed him the most. Bosworth had taken on Davis as a kind of personal charitable project. He knew that many high school jocks faded into school history never to be heard from again. He wanted to make Davis a hard-working, responsible, productive member of society to serve as a role model for other student athletes. To this end he had resisted several attempts by job foremen to have Davis fired for laziness.   Now he saw he should have made his generosity more clear to Davis.   There might still be time.

"Send him in to see me."

Twenty minutes later Ron Davis walked into his office. However this was not the same boy who had come in just over two years ago looking for job.   At that time Davis' face announced that mixture of cockiness and uncertainty that guides most recent high school graduates.   Now the uncertainty was gone.

Davis said nothing and forced Bosworth to talk first. This was one technique he learned from his ACC mentors.   When entering a negotiation or evaluating an offer, the one who speaks first loses.

"Ron, I understand that you and some of your friends have a few problems with working conditions here.   I'd like to listen to what you have to say and see if we can help you out," said Bosworth.

"Well John."   Another technique.   To strip superiority from superiors, address them by first name. Don't use Mr. or any other titles.   Even if your opponent is your mortal enemy, address him as if he is your friend and you have helped to disarm him. "Your employees believe that you do a good job of concentrating on profits but we think we need some representation to concentrate on our best interests as workers."

Bosworth was furious.   Wasn't he known throughout the community as a humanitarian?   Sure he made some healthy profits, but he earned them.   And didn't he use some of his profits to help people?   Everybody knows that don't they?   He lost his cool.

"Goddamn you Davis. I've saved your ass and kept you employed more than once and now you swagger in here to tell me I don't take care of you. You're done. Get out of my company you ungrateful piece of shit."

Davis smiled. Bosworth had lost his composure. It was obvious because both the yelling and the cursing were rare for the man. In fact, probably no one else in the company had ever heard him say "shit." So Davis smiled because he was taught that whenever your opponent loses his composure, smile. It adds to your power and helps you control the situation.

"John, I don't think you want to either fire me or stop the ACC from organizing my working brothers. I have the votes to bring in the ACC. And I have the commitment of enough people that if I walk, they walk and all your contracts will be behind schedule if not lost completely."

"Don't think for a minute that you or any of your cronies are not replaceable. There are many skilled but needy people in this community who would love a job here." Bosworth had regained his composure, but he knew it was too late. He fell back on some of his humanitarian jargon, if for no other reason than to make himself feel better.

"You don't understand," Davis replied evenly. "Just because we walk doesn't mean we walk quietly. We'll make lots of noise, carry lots of signs and attract lots of attention. ACC members from other companies will join us in front of your business and we'll all scream about the injustice heaped on your workers.

"Now, I know you're desperately working to win the contract for the Halsley subdivision. I also know that the Halsley people are very jumpy and don't look kindly on controversy. I think it's safe to say that we can and will block that contract. And if you look for another contract, we'll block that one too. On the other hand, we'll do what we can to help you win the Halsley contract if you allow us to organize formally. I should add that the ACC has some interesting connections with the Halsley corporation."

Bosworth looked at him. "What are you saying?"

"The ACC is already here, in your company. Just not formally...yet. We could try to force ourselves on you, or we can cooperate with you to make this process as smooth as possible. In return for allowing us to organize, we might be able to help you secure the Halsley contract. But no promises," said Davis.

One week later, employees of Bosworth Quality Building quietly voted to make the ACC their union. Two days after that, Bosworth Quality Building was awarded a profitable contract by Halsley Development.

THREE

In the break room of Person's Fine Woodworking, Mitch Person and his four workers were holding a planning session. They worked together like the parts of a Swiss watch, playing well off the thoughts and movements of each other. As their boss, Person led the discussion, but he didn't dominate it. Each employee had equal say in the group's discussions. He admired and respected his employees. They loved him.

In the beginning, Person faced lean times when he left Davis Construction and set out on his own. No major client would consider contracting with a non-union carpenter and facing the political ramifications. And being on his own, Person could not have handled a large project.

Although he would rather have been building castles, Person had to settle for huts. A few meals were missed and all luxuries were foregone, but he was *building*. Things were being constructed by him, to his liking and bearing his mark.

One of his first big contracts was -- ironically, considering his comments when he left his old employer -- a log cabin in the woods. Person was finishing a yard barn for a client when a neighbor approached. The man was old with a wrinkled face the color of a weathered chamois. The sharp eyes looked as if they belonged to a much younger man.

"Tell me young man, why did it take you two days to finish this yard barn? Fred Smithers on the other side of me had his put up last summer and it only took the fella one afternoon to get it in place. I'm guessin' it didn't cost Smithers much either."

"This barn took two days because that's how many were needed," Person replied over his shoulder. He stopped what he was doing, stood, and turned to face the man. "I'm not trying to be a smart alec. I mean just what I say. This barn was designed and built to belong here. It's not just a roof and four walls to keep the lawnmower from rusting. It's now a functioning part of your neighbor's lawn and home."

He pointed two yards over to the other barn the man had mentioned. "That yard barn was designed in a studio somewhere to look attractive in a catalogue or sitting in the parking lot of a big hardware store. If you go five miles in any direction from here, you will see its clones sitting in hundreds of yards. When the owner paid for it, somebody brought out some pre-formed pieces and simply assembled them in his yard. There was no room for craftsmanship on the part of the carpenter. He just pounded some nails to finish what a machine had started in a warehouse somewhere.

"You said it's been in his yard for a year now. Does it fit? Is it part of his yard or is it a distraction? When the owner picked it out did he know the builder was going to stack cinder blocks under one side to keep it level? And on the other side that is just sitting on the ground, has the wood started rotting yet? For his sake, I'm glad he didn't have to wait for it and I hope he didn't pay very much."

The old man listened quietly to Person's monologue. Though his ancient facial features hadn't revealed what he was thinking, his eyes sparkled with amusement.

"I figured your response would be something like that," he said, the corners of his wrinkled mouth turning upward into a sly grin. "I've watched you pretty intently these last couple days, and I have to say I admire the thought and care that goes into your work." The old man didn't say it, but he had been mesmerized by the way Person and his tools became one. It wasn't as if Person used the tool, but as if they used each other to create something worthy of their effort.

He continued, "When I retired several years ago, I bought some land in the forest. My dream has been to have a log cabin built on that property to serve as my final home. Until now, I could not find a man worthy of building it. Would you be interested?"

There was no hesitation.

While building the man's cabin, Person spent several weeks at a time living in an old tent at the work site. The project had been coming together beautifully, and Person was proud, though he would be dirt poor until the cabin was completed and he got paid.

One night he we was eating a can of pork and beans cooked in the can over a small Coleman stove. Mosquitos were biting but he was too exhausted from the day's work to swat them. The moon was out, yet the sky still looked like a large black colander that was letting millions of stars trickle through. Alternating his looks between the sky and the nearly finished cabin that was illuminated by the moon and the stove, Person smiled, lay back on his sleeping bag and thought, "This is what living is all about. I will accept nothing less."

****

With his handsome payment from the completed cabin, Person had enough money to set up a shop in town. Still, no major projects came his way, nor did he seek them. However, word-of-mouth brought in a steady stream of smaller contracts. No matter the project size or its profit margin for him, Person treated each as if it were a palace.

Person's reputation for independence and quality brought not only clients, but also a few prospective employees. Harold Thomas, called Harry Tom by everyone, was the first.

Although he worked a full week, at better pay, for a large, unionized construction firm in town, Harry Tom began working weekends for Person. Thomas asked, begged actually, for a chance to be a part of Person's type of job. A job done for the sake of a job *well* done.

A full week of construction work tends to drain the body of energy, and Thomas usually looked pretty-well exhausted by Friday afternoon. But once involved in one of Person's contracts, where he was given the chance to innovate and excel at his craft, Thomas' fatigue seemed to melt away.

One Saturday, after completing a new room addition for

a local residence, the two men relaxed in the shade of a tree in the back yard, where they could overlook their handiwork. Satisfaction beamed through the sweaty sawdust stuck to their faces.

"Monday through Friday I follow directions, run a saw, pound a nail, whatever," said Harry Tom. "I learned long ago never to try to deviate from written plans or suggest any improvements. Any changes I might make would only screw up one of the other crewmen because he wouldn't recognize that I was trying to improve the project. It's like the attitude of the crew is to complete a project, not to actually create anything. The view is always on the finish line. No one cares how they get there. It's a quota system. Finish a certain number of projects every month and we will all be happy."

"Don't you believe it's important to have goals?" asked Person.

"It depends. Some goals are so shallow that they are more harmful than helpful. I see very little distinction between a construction company that slops together five lousy houses a month and loser who sells drugs to school kids. Both are meeting a goal of making money without any regard to how they are making it," Thomas replied.

Person sat there a moment and smiled. He and Thomas tended to agree on philosophy, especially about work. But he liked to dissect his friend's statements to keep the conversation going. It was better than if they simply agreed with everything the other person said. Their breaks involved as much speech-making and debate as actual rest.

"What's wrong with making money? I like making money," he finally said.

"That's not what I meant," laughed Thomas. He knew his boss was just egging him on. "You know and I know there is a big difference between making money and earning money."

Person chuckled. "I can't help but notice you haven't yet turned back your paychecks to that slop shop you work for during the week. You spend it, but did you earn it?"

Thomas stopped laughing. He knew Person was only teasing him, but sometimes his teasing ripped right through Thomas' day-to-day activities and smacked his true beliefs on the forehead and screamed "Wake up!"

Person ended the awkward moment. "Speaking of paychecks, let's go collect the one for our latest masterpiece."

By the end of the month, Thomas left his other job and began working for Person full time.

The other three employees of Person's Fine Woodworking came to work for Mitchell Person under similar circumstances. Nathan Elders, an African-American, left Davis Construction just a few months after Person and had been jumping restlessly from company to company until he finally found a home in Person's organization. Travis Niles quit the law profession to do something "tangible" with his life. Scott Ramsey, a recent high school graduate, followed Person from a job site he had observed back to Person's shop and begged him for employment.

While none were wealthy, all employees of Person's Fine Woodworking were happy. They shared a love for creation. A love for using their hands and minds to build a lasting testimony to mankind's abilities and his quest for individual excellence. They figured wealth could follow.

In the break room, Person and his crew were discussing upcoming projects and making plans. The winter months were approaching which meant a seasonal drop in work opportunities. In past meetings, the team had devised a budgeting/investment plan that allowed adequate revenue flow during the slow periods. Person, however, was not happy with idle periods. He and his team were discussing options for expanding their operations and bringing in more activity. They were restless, hating the idea of wasting cold months. They wanted to build.

"What's the next step folks?" Person asked.

"We need to focus on aggressive marketing. Let's seek interior renovation jobs in upscale housing," replied Niles. "We've got an excellent reputation among a small group. Now we need to expand. Let's advertise or make phone calls. We'll find some wealthy widow and build her the best stairway she's ever seen or something like that.

"The problem is our location. Quite frankly, anybody with any money will avoid this neighborhood at all costs. No offense, Nate, but this area is the last place a white person with money wants to be."

"You still haven't shed your rich-lawyer mentality yet," said Harry Tom. "There is no glory building something for blue bloods just because they pay you well. I don't feel good about a project unless I think the client feels good about the project.

"The pack mentality of that rich group ruins their ability to appreciate anything for its own sake. They only like something if they think they are supposed to like it. They judge things based on how they think their neighbor will judge things." He sat back and took a sip of his soda. "I don't think I could let myself build something for some old lady who wouldn't appreciate the quality of work that went into it."

As the youngest member of the crew, Scott Ramsey rarely spoke up in these meetings. Generally, he was more interested in absorbing than participating. He made an exception. "I thought one of the reasons we are working for Mitch is to give us chance to do work that we appreciate. Why should we care if the client understands the quality of craftsmanship? Regardless of what I get paid for job, I know I have earned it. Why not get paid more by someone with a lot of money?"

It was Person's turn. "You know, he brings up a good point. We are doing this for ourselves. The benefit of our limited clientele is that they truly appreciate our work. But personally, I don't care if the client can't tell our work from Davis construction stuff. I am satisfied knowing that I did the kind of job that should have been done.

"I'm not interested in forcing the world to appreciate quality workmanship. I'm just looking for a chance to practice quality workmanship and get paid money while I do it. If people don't understand I don't mind...as long as they pay me enough to keep going."

Nate Elders spoke up. "I agree. I would put the same effort into renovating the dump next door as I would into renovating the White House. As long as I got to do the work I want to do and turn a profit, I don't care who the client is. I'm doing this for me."

The team continued to debate the issue among themselves, while Person stared off, not hearing. Something Elders said struck him. Person's shop was located in a rough section of the city. Like most cities, Washington City was faced with drastic economic changes over the past couple of decades. Business relocation to the suburbs led to the deterioration of most of the downtown area. The section which contained Persons's Fine Woodworking was in an especially blighted neighborhood.

City and state leaders had designated the area an enterprise zone with tax breaks and other incentives in an effort to lure businesses back to the area. There was not much success. Most businesses preferred to stay in the suburbs because of lower crime and access to a better-trained workforce.

But Person had little money when he was trying to get established. He needed the lowest-cost facility, and he didn't really care where it was. The price was right on an abandoned shoe factory near downtown. The old red brick building was not in the best of shape, but it provided adequate space for equipment and storage. Thanks to a tax sale by the municipality, some promised renovation on his part, and the enterprise zone incentives, Person now owned the building free and clear. In his usual fasion Person eased into his surroundings, working with the building -- not fighting it -- to transform it into an impressive shop.

As far as a capital investment it wasn't much. Despite its beautiful stature, Person's shop was still in bad surroundings. Its monetary value would always be linked to that of its neighborhood. But Elder's comment made Person think it could be improved.

"Wait a minute," he said, interrupting the debate. All stopped talking and turned to him. "Maybe we look for money next door."

As Travis Niles had explained, Person's Fine Woodworking had trouble getting contracts from wealthy, upper-class clients because the shop was located where few people wanted to visit. The other reason these contracts passed by, though none in the room cared to admit it, was because Person's was a non-union shop. The socialites, many of whom were already self-conscious about their wealth, did not want to associate with non-union organizations. They viewed their dealings with unions as a type of support for the common working man.

The facts were that unions had far more money, influence and political clout than any independent business or chamber of commerce in the state. But the union's PR machines fiercely promoted their image as protector of the little guy. That image was comfortable for the socialites because they could fraternize with the union bosses, who were experienced and cozy with wealth, and still feel as if they were helping the masses.

During the break-room discussion, Person thought that maybe his company should quit competing against the union shops and target a market that they had ignored. He explained his idea to his employees. They agreed to invest their personal savings to try and make it work.

FOUR

Because the state legislature only meets the first few months of each year, lawmakers' offices are pretty modest. The taxpayers' thinking was that since the citizen-legislators only governed part time, they would go back to their real jobs after doing the state's business; therefore, they did not need fancy office space or equipment.

The taxpayers hadn't envisioned Seth Howard.

At the age of 21, the youngest electable age allowed by the state constitution, Seth Howard won his first election to the House of Representatives by outworking his primary and general election opponents. Now, ten years later, Howard was still serving. In fact, as House Majority Leader, he was second in power only to the Speaker of the House. Most Statehouse observers knew, however, that the Speaker was an old, tired man who deferred most of the power-broking to his much younger protégé.

Ten years as a legislator had brought Howard nothing but joy. He was a full-time politician. He had no other job. He had never had another job. He did not ever want another job.

When the legislative session ended for the year in March or April, most of his colleagues returned to teaching, farming or selling real estate. But Howard returned to campaigning, even in non-election years. He never missed a parade or public gathering. His district knew him and liked him and trusted him.

Consequently, most of his district never paid much attention to his activities in the Statehouse. Hardly anyone in his community could tell you how he voted on even the most visible issues, but nearly everyone could reflect on receiving personalized congratulations notes for graduations, marriages, child births, or 50th wedding anniversaries.

Today he sat in his modest chair in his modest office and thought the situation suited him just fine. During his first few terms it was not uncommon for him to sleep in this same office, partly because he worked so late and partly because he didn't have much extra money to pay for a room. It didn't bother him. He would have slept on a bed of rusty nails and broken glass just to be an elected official in a position of power. He was long past the need to sleep in his office, but he kept it under-decorated to maintain a humble image.

Most of his constituents would think his political obsession unnatural, so he always downplayed his love of politics and instead promoted his tireless devotion to serving the public interest. Ironically, he used the unpretentious accommodations provided by stingy taxpayers to show his selfless dedication to public service. Were his quarters too posh, the voters might have suspected his motives. Besides, as long as he had access to a phone and a staff he could accomplish what he needed. He didn't usually need fancy surroundings.

Sometimes, voters liked their elected officials to appear as statesmen. Thanks to speaking fees and some interesting campaign finance loopholes, Howard had acquired the means to dress well and travel conspicuously when the situation called for it. He always knew whether the public-servant or powerful-statesman image would be appropriate and he appeared accordingly.

Politics and power were his true fuel. In his successful career he pointed to two cunning moves that put him in his current enviable position: aligning himself with the frail man that now controlled the Speaker's gavel, and forging a relationship with union PAC money.

The first move allowed him to make or break political careers in the state. Therefore, he could summon a line of lawmakers willing to do his bidding at any time.

The second, coupled with his own aggressive incumbency efforts, made him virtually unbeatable in his district. Seth Howard was around as long as he damn well pleased.

The phone rang. Howard looked at his watch. Right on time, he thought.

He picked up the receiver. "The ACC stands for Assholes, Crooks and Crybabies."

There was a brief pause on the other end, followed by Ron Davis trying to disguise his voice and failing miserably. "How dare you," he said in a falsetto. "I'm just some poor widow trying to get help locating my welfare check."

"It's lying there next to your bottle of bourbon," Howard replied.

Davis laughed. Back to his normal voice, "You sure like to take chances that it's me and not some poor slob who votes for you."

"Hey, the legislature is out until next year. The only people calling me at my desk are people who want to be contributors or contributors who want to be people.

"You're a long-time friend and contributor, so I guess you want to pretend like you're some poor working stiff who is being abused by the system."

"The system worked fine 'til you politicians started fucking things up," Davis laughed again.

Both men were in a jovial mood. They knew Davis would ask a favor and Howard would grant it. This is the way business had been conducted for the better part of a decade.

A week later, a memo was circulated around the supervisors at Davis Construction. It was from Ron Davis himself, congratulating his company for winning the bid for the new multi-million dollar state government office building.

FIVE

"You the gentlemen looking for a printer?" The African-American face was rough but clean. His sharp eyes studied Person, Thomas and Elders carefully as he entered the newly renovated print shop.

"Yes sir. Please come in," Thomas answered.

The man walked toward the desk slowly but deliberately. He lived about a block from this building. Sadly, he had watched the area deteriorate gradually over the years until it became an abandoned, vandalized shell of a shopping center typical of many inner-city neighborhoods.

He watched with some amusement when the white man opened Person's Fine Woodworking in the corner building that once housed a small shoe factory. He watched more intently when the white man and his partners started renovating the old shop next door to their factory. When the "Print shop -- help wanted" sign was hung on the door he decided it was time to introduce himself to his new neighbors.

As he walked across the room, he took in the renovation work the men had done. He admired the quality and the attention to detail.

For most of the day, a steady stream of African-Americans from the neighborhood had been flowing into the new print shop. Nate Elders predicted this would happen, explaining to Person the chronic unemployment in these areas. Most of the people, he said, wanted to work but didn't have the transportation or skills to find meaningful jobs outside their depressed neighborhoods. Many would have enough raw talent that they would be worth training.

Some good prospects came in today, but the man in their shop now stood out. He carried himself with an air of confidence, shoulders straight, eyes looking directly at everything and everyone, no hesitation in his step. Person silently noted that although the man's clothes were not especially nice, they were clean, pressed and likely the best clothes the man owned. It was clear he intended to impress his potential employers... if they lived up to his own expectations.

The three construction workers respected his attitude.

During the ensuing conversation, they learned he was Rudolph Jefferson. He had lived in this neighborhood most of his adult life. Though he was unemployed now, he had worked a myriad of jobs over the years, including a couple of different stints at some print shops in town.

When they inquired as to why he never seemed to hold any one job for very long he looked them straight in the eye and remained silent for what must have been several minutes. It was as if he was trying to determine if they were worthy of the truth.

Apparently, he believed they were. "I've worked hard at a variety of jobs for a variety of bosses," he began. "In every case I've made the same mistake that always seems to lead to me being fired or made uncomfortable enough to quit. I always do more than I am asked to do.

"I don't mean just plain working hard or being willing to put in overtime. Those things have always been rewarded. It's when I go one step further that things get messed up. After working someplace a while I usually see ways to make things run better. But when I make suggestions to my supervisors they either treat me like I can't possibly know what I'm talking about because I'm Black, or they get that scared look in their eye that says they know I'm right, but they sure as hell don't want some nigger to get the credit for something they should've thought of.

"Either way, my ideas don't get put in place. Maybe I should just let 'em slide, but I never do. I can't. Once I see there's a better way, I can't stand doing it the old way. I know the job won't change, so I move on."

He had never talked this openly about his frustrations with anyone. But for some reason he could not exactly explain, he felt he could trust the men in the room with him. So he continued.

"You asked about my job experiences. I'll tell you. I show up and apply for a job. I don't have the schooling to get into an office so I have to try for a labor job.

"Usually, the places I go are looking to hire some Blacks to fill out quotas, so I always have a pretty good chance at getting a job. When I'm hired I work hard and I do a good job. I usually work longer hours and do better than any of my co-workers. I'm not trying to show anybody up; it's just my nature to work that way.

"Like I said before, sooner or later I spot something that

could be done better, a change for the assembly line, an idea for a new tool, something like that. I can't describe how I always recognize what should be done. And I can't explain why it's always me who sees it. I consider it a talent, though it's treated me like it's a curse.

"Anyway, I take my suggestion to my supervisor and he says something back. It doesn't matter what words he uses, what he's saying to me is, 'Look nigger, we hired you to keep the civil rights people off our backs. Don't come in here and act like you run the place.'

"The first couple times it really bothered me. Now it's almost funny. Even though I know it'll cost me my job, I go back time and again and keep bringing up the same issue. I go back until they either listen to me or fire me. One day, I expect, someone will actually listen to me, but it hasn't happened yet.

"So that's the 'mistake' I made in the past and will make in the future. If you gentlemen hire me for your print shop, you'll probably fire me for the same reasons the other people fired me. To tell the truth, I don't really care. I'm used to it.

"It's not the most convenient way to live, but it's the only way I can live. This has never been good for my wallet, but it's kept my soul intact. That's what I care about."

For a few moments nobody said anything. Person looked around at his partners. Knowing what their leader was thinking, they nodded in agreement.

"Mr. Jefferson, we want to offer you the position of executive manager of our new print shop," Person said. "But before you accept or decline I want to explain our goals so you know exactly what you're getting into.

"My colleagues and I are builders. We create. We live our lives to demonstrate what we, as individuals, are able to achieve. To create something that is worthy of being a monument to mankind's greatness is our drive. Whether small or large, every project we complete must stand as a testimony of what humanity can produce to serve itself.

"Until now, our material of choice has been wood. Today, we are expanding. Our new material will be commerce. We will use commerce to rebuild this neighborhood.

"Don't be mistaken. We are not aiming to help you or anyone else. We are not striving for praise from politicians and community leaders. Our motive is much stronger. Profit.

"I own the building next door. My business is successful and my colleagues and I have worked hard to earn an adequate living. But I want the building and the business to be worth more. If we bring commerce into this neighborhood, the value of my building and business will increase. It's very simple really.

"Our plan is this: My colleagues and I are pooling our resources to buy this nearly worthless real-estate one building at a time. In each building we will start a new business. If the business is successful, we will sell the business to the executive manager and use some of those profits to invest in the next building. If not, we will close the business and try something else.

"Like I said before, our material is commerce and the only good way to tell if commerce is working is if we turn a profit.

"If you want the job, it will be your responsibility to see that the print shop is profitable. As owners, we will provide equipment and train you how to manage this store. We will be able to use our experience to provide input into business decisions, but those decisions will ultimately be yours.

"If those decisions are good ones, the business will one day be yours. If they are bad decisions, we will sell the equipment and cut our losses and you will be looking for another job."

Person waited a minute to let it all sink in. "What do you think?"

"Why would you look for profit here?" Jefferson asked. "Most folks gave up on this place a long time ago. Why should I take that chance that we can make a profit when nobody else could before?"

Elders spoke up. "It's easier to make a profit when you start out with such low overhead. These buildings can be had for a song. Equipment is expensive, but equipment is created to help good people get more product out of their effort. If we can find the right people to put behind the equipment then we can make a profit.

"We're taking a chance in looking in a bad neighborhood for good workers. But we figure there are plenty of strong, decent Black men and women who haven't been able to move out yet because of prejudice, bad luck or some other reason. No other business is recruiting here, so we get to pick the cream of the crop."

"There ain't much cream around here. Mostly sour milk," Jefferson said. "Hell, I ain't working anywhere else. Might as well give this a shot."

****

The print shop got off to a slow start. Jefferson would not even open for business for the first few weeks, preferring to spend all his time mastering the presses to his satisfaction.

Eventually, Jefferson knew everything about operating and repairing each piece of equipment in his shop. That accomplished, he borrowed some of Person's business forms and contracts, made some interesting innovations in both appearance and function of those forms and asked Person to become his first client.

Earlier, Person explained to Jefferson that, despite Person's vested interest in the success of the print shop, he was satisfied with his current printer, so Jefferson would need to earn Person's business if he wanted it.

Person was impressed with Jefferson's work. It would be difficult to describe exactly why the new forms were better than the old ones. The changes were subtle. But Jefferson's forms were more pleasing to look at. Each form was designed so that, regardless of how complicated the language might be, you felt like you knew exactly how to fill it out.

And the letterhead logo seemed like it belonged on the page. Person's current printer used the same basic form for everybody and merely changed the logo at the top of the page. Jefferson's design made the form and logo go together. It neither stood out like a full-color afterthought, nor did it blend in with the rest of the text. Again, you couldn't exactly point to why it looked better, it just did.

Person took one of the new contracts and filled it out to make Jefferson his new printer.

Now that he had some money coming in, Jefferson put a sign on the door and began pounding the pavement in search of clients. He decided to name his new shop "Brother's Printing." This name, he believed, would give his shop an image of warmth and trust among the general public. Among his fellow African-Americans, it would tell who was running the show.

It turned out that he had to depend on the second group to get the business rolling. Even dressed in a new suit and armed with his new forms, Jefferson had trouble getting clients. He could tell that the businessmen he met liked his forms, but they wouldn't buy. The deals were lost once his black face walked into the room.

It didn't take many disappointments to make Jefferson change tactics and focus on the few African-American-owned businesses in town. With those, he was extremely successful. Brother's Printing took off, allowing Jefferson to start hiring employees from his neighborhood.

His clients, including Person, reported that the new forms had actually been the deciding factor in winning contracts for their own businesses. As word spread, so did Brother's Printing. Even white-owned companies put aside earlier prejudice and became customers.

Person sold the shop to Jefferson at a healthy profit. The plan was working.

Next, they started a painting company, followed by a welding shop, then a plumbing company. The common thread running through each operation was an absolute devotion to quality. Each company was successful because the executive manager had to produce a product that was so obviously superior that the business could overcome its disadvantaged location.

Although business experts say the three most important keys to business success are location, location and location, they are usually talking about retail businesses, where customers must come to you. All the new shops took their products to the customer.

As the small business district was being reclaimed from the urban nightmare surrounding it, a few investors began to take notice and purchase property for their own businesses. Person did not mind, because the new investments helped increase the value of the property he already held.

Soon, Mitchell Person and his fellow investors were wealthy men.

<u>SIX</u>

Sandy Davis sat at her desk, sweater over her shoulders, clutching a fresh cup of coffee to try and keep warm. She wasn't much of a coffee drinker, but her desk area was always cold, and she discovered that holding a fresh cup of coffee helped keep her hands warm. Usually, she emptied her mug once the coffee cooled and re-filled for a new steaming cup.

She faced this problem every time the weather started to turn cold. Some areas of the building were ignored by the building's heating system. Other parts, however, were sweltering. In the summer, it was just the opposite. The hot spots became cold spots and the cold spots baked.

Her dad built this building and she hated it. It wasn't just the heating and cooling system. The roof leaked. The basement smelled musty. And the layout of office and desk space made the workers feel like Orwellian prisoners. If a building could ever be responsible for low employee morale, this was the building.

She couldn't believe it when she found out her dad won the contract for the new state office building. Actually, she was never shocked anymore when her father was awarded something he didn't deserve. But this time she figured it was obvious that his last office building was so poor that he couldn't possibly be considered for another one.

Obviously, she thought, there were forces at work other than competence and performance.

Had she been on the State Office Building Commission, she told herself, she would have made certain that Ron Davis didn't so much as hammer one nail in the new building. Ironically, she could have been on that commission if she told her dad she wanted it. With his government contacts, he could make one phone call and she could have any government job she wanted. Of course, she then would have paybacks to fulfill if any of his business came before the state.

She didn't want her life to be a series of favors from and to her dad. Instead, she went about things her own way, and now was one of the least glamorous of state employees. Social worker.

Her dad hadn't been happy with her choice of careers. After all, he sent her to the best schools and gave her everything she wanted. He expected her to be a high-priced lawyer, surgeon or community leader. But she used her expensive education to get a job that paid her just slightly more than the earnings of the poverty-level clients she served.

She smiled to herself when she imagined her father wandering around his study, scratching his head and trying to figure out why his daughter was so much trouble. She didn't get any pleasure from tormenting her dad, but she figured it was good for him. Her brothers all acquiesced to his demands too easily.

Sandy wore her brown hair short and plain. Her clothes

weren't on the cutting edge of anything, and she rarely wore makeup. Yet she was still very pretty to those who bothered to give her a second look. Though they got along with Sandy very well, the other women in her office snickered behind her back about her plain clothes and looks, but each of them secretly hoped she would never start making an effort at beauty. Even a small effort would increase their competition considerably.

Despite her nonchalance about fashion and face cream, she liked to date. Between her own finds and the bozos her father set her up with, she went out on the town quite a bit. No serious relationships yet.

Right now, however, she was not thinking about men. Over the past few days, Sandy had been contacting some of her cases to tell them they were no longer eligible for some of the available welfare programs. This was always the most frustrating part of her job.

To her, it was as if her job duties contradicted themselves. She helped needy citizens fill out forms and go through all the necessary paperwork to qualify for public assistance. Then she tried to help them find jobs, finish school or do whatever they needed to improve their quality of life.

But once they found a job and started earning an income, she had to withdraw public assistance. The problem was that the benefits from the entry-level jobs that most of her cases qualified for could not match the benefits provided by the welfare system. When her clients discovered what they would lose if they continued to work, many quit to get back on the public plan, especially those who had families to support. Only a rare few took the chance that their employer-provided benefits would increase over time.

The problem as she saw it was that the public assistance, particularly health care, was too good. The public health care program for needy people started out as a basic plan, but over the years the program kept expanding and expanding. The culprits were the lobbyists for health care groups that want the enormous amounts of public money that pay the bills for the needy, and the politicians who try to buy the votes of the lower-class.

This angered her. The idea of public assistance got mucked up to the point that it was doing more harm than good. Were they helping people get back on their feet or were they creating dependents who could never get back on their feet? Whenever government starts fighting against its own goals, it's time to either change the goals or change the system, she thought. Perhaps, she wondered, the goals had already been changed.

At times she felt guilty working for this screwed up system. Although the law only required her to notify her clients by mail that they were being pulled from the welfare rolls, she tried to call the ones who had phones. Not all caseworkers did this, but she felt it was important to try and talk to her people, answer their questions and help them work through their frustration.

Even with her masters degree she had trouble understanding why the system worked the way it did. She could not expect her clients, most with just a high school equivalency, to understand why they were suddenly being "punished" for trying to become productive members of society.

Some people yelled. Some cried. Some cursed. And

some just became silent and hung up. However, in the last month a new response had her puzzled. Three people actually laughed at her. It wasn't a laugh of frustration or pending insanity. It was genuine amusement.

As she studied the files of her laughing clients, she found a few similarities. All were African-American, but so were 90 percent of her clients, so that didn't help her. All were from the same inner-city neighborhood, again not unique. All found jobs without her help. Hmm.

In helping her clients find work, Sandy used a list of businesses that had hired hard-luck cases in the past. Nearly all her cases that found jobs were hired by one of these businesses. These three men were different. Two worked for a painting company she had never heard of and the third for a print shop. Both companies were located in the same neighborhood where the men lived. Remarkably, the men's salaries were better than the starting wage paid by any of the businesses on her list.

Recognizing that the businesses were in an enterprise zone, she got up to do some investigating at the department of commerce. She left her sweater at her desk because the department of commerce was in one of the hot areas of the building.

One of her former suitors worked in the enterprise zone division. She and Bob Hanlon had gone out a few times, but they lost romantic interest in each other pretty quickly. No particular reason. It just happened that way. The break-off was mutual so they were still good friends.

"Hey Bob, how are things in the tropics?" She noted the fan by his desk.

"Balmy. How's the North Pole?"

"We're planning a dog-sled race this afternoon. Want to watch?"

"No thanks," he laughed. "What can I do for you?"

The climate of the building was a common joke between them. He knew he could bitch about it without offending her. Some other state employees wrongly assumed that she would be upset knowing people criticized the building her dad built.

"What can you tell me about the Laughton Park enterprise zone?"

"Nothing off the top of my head. We have about 70 zones. Most were created to give tax breaks to major campaign contributors, others to let inner-city politicians take credit for trying to bring jobs to their area. I think Laughton Park was one of the second kind."

As he was talking, he walked to a large filing cabinet and started digging. "Here we go," he said and pulled out a folder.

"Yeah, this is one of the Seth-Howard-the-humanitarian enterprise zones. He gets these things through the legislature periodically to throw a bone to his constituents. He represents some of the worst parts of the city, but he loves it because they walk into the voting booth and pull his lever without thinking. He wins those neighborhoods with about 85 percent of the vote.

"Thing is, these zones rarely pan out. The tax breaks are nice, but no business in its right mind would move in. The neighborhood is still crappy you know. Seth gets the zones in place, makes a bunch of speeches, but he never follows up. Hmm, this is odd,"

"What is it?" Sandy asked.

But Hanlon didn't answer. He just kept studying the forms in the file and mumbling to himself.

Finally he replied, "It seems several businesses have started up in the past couple of years. Maybe Seth Howard has brought jobs to the area after all. Except...Hmm." He continued to look through the file.

Sandy patiently waited for him to continue.

"All but a couple of these applications for tax breaks were filled out by a Mitchell Person. Ever heard of him?"

"No. But I wouldn't hear about him unless he were either destitute, or some goon my dad wanted me to marry."

"Oh what a shame I never got to meet your dad," he said sarcastically.

"He wouldn't have liked you."

"His loss. Anyway, it looks like this Person guy is growing his own little empire right in the heart of hell. Could be a rich friend of Seth's that's been put up to create some quick jobs in the area before the next election. I heard Seth has been running a little scared lately because he thinks an African-American might run against him in the primary. I doubt anybody would be stupid enough to run against Seth Howard, but Seth doesn't take chances."

"It could be something else. Maybe one of the locals opened shop to launder drug money," said Sandy.

"Want me to check into it some more? I could call one of Seth's staffers and see if he knows anything about it."

"No thanks. I'd rather check it out first hand."

"I wouldn't go alone. It's not a nice neighborhood. Want me to tag along?"

"I'll be fine. Remember, I work with people in that neighborhood. Some I know on a first-name basis."

After getting copies of the Laughton Park file and thanking Hanlon for his help, Sandy left to get her coat. She planned a drive-by investigation for that afternoon.

****

Re-election was a year-round job for Seth Howard. He was usually pretty busy in the Statehouse, but he still scheduled plenty of district visits.

Today he was the luncheon speaker for a Westside Teachers Association meeting. He was running behind, so he was feverishly pouring over his speech notes while his driver raced him to the restaurant where the meeting was held.

Knowing a short-cut, the driver cut through the Laughton Park neighborhood. At one corner, he noticed a bunch of redevelopment projects taking place. The buildings were clean, the boards were off the windows, and businesses were actually open.

"That's new," he thought. He turned to see if Seth had noticed, but the lawmaker was still wrapped up in speech preparation. The driver was about to say something, but thought better of distracting his boss.

They made it to the speech on time and Seth Howard did a wonderful job.

After the speech, the driver took the normal, safer route back to the office. By they time they got back, the driver had forgotten about Laughton Park.

<u>SEVEN</u>

"I'm sorry Ron. If I could change Tom's mind I would. I've tried everything I can think of but he's set on awarding the contract to this other guy," Al Trent was speaking into his phone in a low tone. His boss was about to award a construction contract to a company other than Davis Construction. To make matters worse, it was going to a non-union firm. Al felt obligated to call Ron Davis and give him advance warning, even though Al could get fired for leaking this information ahead of time.

"Goddamn it!" Davis yelled into his end of the phone. "Put Tom on the phone and let me talk to him."

"No no no," he said in a panicky whisper, glancing around to make sure no one was within earshot. "He'd have my ass if he knew I was on the phone with you right now. He's not going to announce the contract for another few days and he wants this kept secret. But we're old friends. I thought you should know."

"Yeah. I'm sorry buddy. I didn't mean to yell," Ron Davis softened his tone. He needed more information and he knew he wouldn't get it if he panicked his source. "So, who's getting the job?"

"A smaller firm in town. This will probably be the biggest job they ever did," Trent looked down at his notes. "Person's Fine Woodworking. Ever hear of 'em?"

Davis thought for a moment. The name sounded familiar, but he couldn't place it. "I'm not sure. What'd they bid?"

"They undercut you by a significant amount. I think it's because they pay below union scale," Trent said. "Tom said he likes their, um," he flipped back through his notes to find the exact quote. "Their 'fresh approach, like the project was ordained from God.' Whatever the hell that means.

"I tried to reason with the man. I tried to get him to see the benefits of hiring union, but he wouldn't listen. Despite his ordained from God shit, I think he can't look past the bottom line. Sorry."

"Thanks, Al. I know you did what you could." Nonchalantly, Davis added. "When is Tom going to make the announcement?"

"Tuesday morning."

They said their goodbyes and hung up. Davis picked up his receiver again and made a few quick calls. Tuesday afternoon, he and a few of his friends were going to dump the stock they held in Al Trent's employer, Behnam United. They didn't hold enough stock to sink the company, but they could lower the price enough to make Tom Behnam and the other stockholders nervous.

He knew this action would send a subtle but clear message to other major companies not to mess with Ron Davis.

Now he turned his attention to two other matters.

First, he needed to figure out how to keep these non-union

shops from underbidding ACC companies. For government contracts, the problem was solved. A few years ago, he and Seth Howard had used Seth's political arm-twisting and a few of Davis' well-placed campaign donations to pass a prevailing wage law for government contracts.

This law required companies bidding for government contracts to pay their employees the "prevailing wage." This was interpreted by the Department of Administration, rife with friends of Davis, to mean the current union wage.

Once the competition was in the same ballpark as Davis Construction, Ron knew no one could undercut him by very much if at all. Then, he could manipulate his friends to make sure his bid was accepted.

The problem was with private-sector companies. Davis and Howard had been successful in broadening the interpretation of the government prevailing wage law to apply to private companies that received government money, but they were having trouble passing a prevailing wage law that covered completely independent companies.

Recently, Davis had lost more than one major bid on projects with private-sector companies. It was time to work on the prevailing wage law again.

Also, he needed to check out Person's Fine Woodworking.

****

Although none of her friends would come near this neighborhood, Sandy Davis felt relatively safe here. She had been mugged once, but before it was over, three of her clients saw what was happening, jumped on the attacker, and got her purse back.

No matter how poor in wealth or spirit her welfare clients were, she tried to treat them with respect. Many of them, including her three saviors that day, reacted favorably to her treatment. Some genuinely liked her, despite her being part of the establishment.

She didn't push her luck by coming here at night. If she got out of her car, she didn't leave the keys in the ignition. Nor did she wear fancy clothes and flash wads of money. But she could usually conduct her business without harassment.

Today's business was just a drive-by. She planned to drive in, look at the new developments, and drive out.

When she got to the block where the new Laughton Park businesses were located, plans changed. She had to get out of the car and take a closer look.

It didn't look like a few businesses had been opened up in some old crappy buildings for a few months merely to create some pre-election jobs. Rather, the entire block looked different, in a permanent way.

She had trouble describing to herself what the difference was. It was cleaner, of course, but there was something else about this business district. It looked kind of like an organism of commerce. Each business was distinct, but at the same time, every business belonged to the block. A hand and a foot serve different functions, but each is part of the body. This is how the new business district looked to her.

She parked in front of Person's Fine Woodworking and got out.

Harry Tom just finished turning a spindle on the shop lathe, when he looked up and saw the attractive woman walking in the front door. She was tall, slender, and walked with an air of confidence that made the room seem to move around her. It appeared as if she dressed down and refused makeup in an attempt to hide her beauty. It didn't work.

Eagerly, he removed his safety goggles and approached her.

"Hi. What can I do for you?," he asked.

Sandy jumped and turned to look at him. She had been admiring the inside of this shop and was startled to hear a voice directed at her. There were plenty of people in the shop, and plenty of noise, but all the din seemed an integral part of production. It seemed no more natural for a person to speak to her than for a hammer or table saw to speak to her.

"Uh, is Mr. Person here?"

"I was afraid you would say that," Harry Tom responded, trying to portray the look of one who's had his heart broken. "Once again the lowly worker loses out to the boss."

She relaxed somewhat and smiled with a look that said she was amused at his performance, but not interested.

"I don't have an appointment or anything, but I'd like to see him. Oh," she extended her hand. "I'm Sandy Davis, with the Department of Human Services."

He accepted her handshake. "Harry Tom. You won't

need an appointment. He's right back here."

As they walked back to the office, it occurred to Sandy for the first time that if she walked into Person's office, she would have to actually say something to him. Right now, she had no idea what it would be.

Harry Tom led her to the office, made the introductions and went back to the shop. On the way back it hit him that this was the first time he had ever seen a younger woman anywhere near Mitch. He had spent a lot of time with Person both professionally and personally, and the only women he had ever seen around Person were old widowed clients.

"It's funny," he thought, "but I never thought of that before now. He's successful. He's not a bad-looking guy as far as I can tell. Yet, I've never seen him with a date." After a minute or two, Harry Tom decided that Mitch Person was asexual, if anything, that he didn't need to worry about it, and that he should get back to work.

In Mitch Person's office, Sandy Davis was intimidated for the first time in her life.

If she could credit her father with one important lesson, it was how to always keep the upper hand when dealing with people. Like her dad, she had a knack for always knowing what subtle buttons to push so she was always in control of the situation. This time, her lessons failed her.

This man before her was staring directly into her being, into her soul. She had never felt so stripped of her defenses. Had she been standing, naked, before a room full of men, she would have felt more comfortable than she felt right now.

She blushed, stammered, shifted her weight back and forth, and he just stood patiently. Waiting.

After an eternity, which was probably closer to ten seconds, she said, "I, uh. Thanks for seeing me (boy, was that an accurate statement). Well, I guess I haven't prepared exactly what I want to say..."

Person cut her off. "I know a few of my employees have been taken off the welfare roles. If you are here to get them back, I can assure you they are not interested."

Finally, she remembered why she was here. "No, no, no," she laughed. "I'm here out of curiosity. It's rare enough that I take someone off welfare for reasons other than death. It's even more rare when those people actually thank me for doing so. I'm interested in why."

Person studied her for a minute. "I am not a spokesman for anyone but myself. I would guess it has something to do with the fact that they are using their minds and bodies to accomplish something. They are getting paid for their accomplishments rather than for their patience with bureaucracy. But you'd have to ask them if you want to know for sure."

"Actually, I wasn't planning to spend much time here today. I may want to ask some more questions later," she said as she was backing toward the door. "Do you have a card?"

She glanced at the card. Then did a double-take. What a good-looking card, she thought. I wonder who printed it.

"Thanks for your time Mr. Person," she said.

"Call me Mitch. Am I in some kind of official trouble?"

"No. Like I said, I'm just curious. It looks like you are

doing something wonderful here." As an afterthought she added, "I don't know where Seth Howard found you, but you can tell him he's got my vote."

He watched her leave. As he went back to his desk, he thought, "Who's Seth Howard?"

EIGHT

Late Tuesday morning, Person called Harry Tom, Nate Elders, Travis Niles and Scott Ramsey into the break room and shut the door behind them. When they sat down, he took out a box of expensive cigars, placed it in the middle of the table and opened it.

"These are for everybody, but I wanted to make sure each of you had a chance to get one."

They sat for a moment looking at Person.

Then Niles blurted, "The Benham United bid!"

"Congratulations," said Person.

Bedlam, or as much as five men can create, erupted in the break room. Cigars were lit, high fives were exchanged, and whoops and hollers were emitted.

A few of the other workers began to gather around the break room, peeking in the window, wondering what was going on. They would find out soon enough. And that day, the atmosphere at Person's Fine Woodworking was even more proud, and somewhat smokier, than usual.

****

Sandy sat at her desk and shivered more than normal. It wasn't just the cold. It was the stare, too. She couldn't shake Mitch Person's piercing eyes. They followed her to work. They followed her home. They followed her in the shower. And they kept her sleep restless.

She told herself it was just professional curiosity in the redevelopment of Laughton Park. She told herself that, but she wasn't very convincing.

Clearly, Mitch Person had not set up shop to launder drug money. Also, the businesses were lasting, not just facades for the election year. But why had he chosen that bad area for development? And how had he succeeded?

Deciding she wouldn't answer those questions today, she turned back to her other duties and tried to ignore the stare, lurking in the shadows of her thoughts.

****

"What a shithole," thought Ron Davis as he looked at the listed address of Person's Fine Woodworking. As a man who liked to know as much as possible about the people he dealt with, Davis kept a private investigator on a retainer. The PI was slimy, yet thorough. Davis liked that.

This report on Mitchell Person was the usual good job. It included a summary page of vital statistics like name, address, phone numbers, romantic interests, etc. The rest of the file was filled with all the details.

Typically, Davis wouldn't bother looking past the summary page if he didn't think it would be worth his time. After seeing the Laughton Park address of shop, he was about to toss the folder aside, thinking the Benham United bid was just a fluke. Then he saw the "Estimated net worth" listing.

Slowly, he began to study the file. Person's company's net worth didn't begin to approach that of Davis Construction, but it was much larger than it should have been for any kind of business in the lousy part of town. This guy deserved a closer look.

A half-hour later, Davis set the file aside and leaned back in his chair to think.

He was somewhat shocked to find out that Person used to work for him. Now it looked like he was making a respectable business for himself with a non-union shop. To make matters worse, he was the beneficiary of Seth Howard's tax breaks. In the report, the PI suggested that perhaps there was some tie between Howard and Person, that perhaps Howard was trying to secretly steal part of Davis' construction business.

Davis doubted that. But it was interesting. Obviously, Howard would have to know about any major redevelopment in his district, so why hadn't mentioned anything to Davis? The two men respected each other and considered themselves friends. But each knew better than to completely trust the other.

Davis picked up the phone and dialed Howard's office.

<u>NINE</u>

Mitch Person was distracted, and it bothered him. He thought he could always focus on his work. That was the one constant in his life. The thing he could count on.

Right now, there was plenty of work to concentrate on. The Benham United projectstarted extremely well, despite some early stock market jitters. Smaller projects continued to pour into his shop. And the other Laughton Park business were exceeding expectations.

He should have been elated, but he wasn't. All this activity to keep him busy, yet *that woman* kept creeping into his mind.

Since he started his own business, he had made sure no woman would get in the way of what he wanted. Quite frankly, he couldn't remember his last date. And he wasn't particularly interested in starting that game again.

He tried to blank her out of his thoughts, but the harder he worked, the more his mind wandered back to that tall, slender siren, with the plain looks. No, "plain" wasn't accurate. She didn't wear makeup or do anything special with her hair, but anything she did would have only covered her true beauty.

People don't try to mess with the smile of the Mona Lisa. Nor do they round the corners and re-proportion a woman in a Picasso masterpiece. Some things are better untouched.

"Yes, that's it," he thought as he smiled. "She's a masterpi...Dammit there I go again." His smile faded. He crinkled his brow and tried to concentrate on the papers in front of him.

After a few minutes, he threw the papers aside, frustrated, and reached for the phone book. Thumbing through the government pages he mumbled, "Sandy Davis, health and human services."

He reached for the phone.

****

Seth Howard was embarrassed and looking for someone to blame. He just got off the phone with Ron Davis, who was quizzing him about some activity in the Laughton Park enterprise zone. He had to admit to his friend and his main campaign contributor that he did not know what was going on in his own enterprise zone in his own district.

Not very impressive from a legislator who likes to boast of being in touch with the people.

He planned to take a big bite out of a staff member's ass, but sensing his frame of mind, his staff all found "important" errands to run out of the office while he was on the phone. He couldn't find anybody to holler at. They would be back when they figured he had time to cool down.

What the hell was going on in that enterprise zone? He didn't want anything to happen there. He hated enterprise zones.

Enterprise zones created tax breaks, and he was against anything that would cut tax revenues. A few tax breaks might create a few jobs to employ a few people, but taxes gave him a lot of money to help a lot of people. His help turned into their votes.

The way he saw it, corporate tax breaks didn't create new businesses. If the tax advantage enticed a company to relocate from a suburb to downtown then there would be no significant creation of jobs and a real net loss of tax dollars. Property tax breaks merely cut the potential public revenue from the area base (overlooking the fact that even reduced taxes paid by thriving businesses were better than the taxes generated from abandoned buildings).

He preferred the tax revenue to the tax breaks. In fact he had carefully chosen Laughton Park and the other enterprise zones he pushed through the legislature because he figured no one would ever use them. But that did not stop him from skillfully using the enterprise-zone rhetoric he didn't believe.

For him, these areas were a win-win situation. Since they were located where unemployment was highest, he could tell the local residents that he was working to create jobs. And because the zones where in the worst areas of the city, he was confident that no business would actually come in there and lessen its obligation to the state treasury.

He had used tactics like this to make quite a name for himself around the state as the savior of the little guy. He was famous for his stump speeches where he criticized big business for trying to cheat the taxpayers out of benefits that were rightfully theirs. He talked about how corporations hired high-priced accountants so they wouldn't have to pay any taxes, denying important education, food and medical care to the other citizens of the state. But, by God, Seth Howard and his political party would close those tax loopholes to make big business pay its fair share, he would say.

Of course, when he went into a district to boast about another enterprise zone or similar job creation effort, nobody ever pointed out that he was suddenly in favor of business. Either people didn't notice the contradiction, or they were too polite to mention it. Seth Howard had been in politics long enough to realize that voter apathy was the likely cause.

Now, some asshole had moved into *his* enterprise zone in *his* district and started employing *his* voters without talking with *him* first. Seth Howard was not happy.

TEN

After she hung up the phone, Sandy sat still at her desk, even forgetting to shiver. She stared at the receiver resting in its cradle.

He called. The man who, just a few days ago, violated her inner soul with his intent gaze called to offer her another chance to submit.

Actually, he had invited her for a more thorough tour of the Laughton Park redevelopment. It was innocent enough, but she figured that he knew that he invaded her mind with just a short visit. Now he wanted to become a part of her every conscious moment.

Maybe he was some kind of parasite that fed on the breakdown of strong women. She agreed to meet him anyway. That afternoon.

Sandy Davis did not believe in love or infatuation, especially at first sight. She did believe in lust, though she had only experienced it a few times before.

This guy was different. She had only met him briefly, so it couldn't be love. Yet she couldn't shake the thought of him. It was time to see him again, to convince herself that it was just a weird emotional feeling, brought on by an expectation to find a drug dealer or political crony.

One more meeting would set her mind straight. Besides, she was genuinely interested in his redevelopment activities.

Now that she had come to grips with this "passing fancy" she could relax. Her drive to Laughton Park was actually quite pleasant. She managed most of the trip without thinking about him.

When she approached Mitchell Person's block, though, things changed. He was nearly a block away, standing outside his shop, but it was as though he were directly in front of her. There were other people on the street, but he stood out, and it wasn't only because of his white, though tanned, face.

Rather, he was like a part of the buildings and their activities that temporarily extended out onto the sidewalk to beckon her. Something about the way he stood, the way he carried himself, made it obvious that he was a part of the redevelopment around him, and it was a part of him.

It wasn't his clothing that made him look in charge, it was more his persona. He wore faded jeans, and stood with his hands in the pockets of a light jacket that fought the fall wind that tousled his dark, unruly hair.

As she parked the car, her composure returned. Her initial impressions were replaced by curiosity and wonder, enabling her to study and analyze this man. These feelings were more comfortable to her. Once the emotions were set aside and she could settle into her analytical process, she could focus on the man and his surroundings and what made them unique.

They extended their greetings, and Mitch started her tour. He began with his original construction shop, which was mostly empty because all available hands were working at the Benham United project. He explained that until they could hire all the quality workers they needed, all other projects were put on hold so his entire staff could work at the Benham site. He said he had been there since sunrise, but made a special trip back to keep this appointment.

She noticed the dirt under his nails and the filthy lines on his face left from where sweat had collected dust and run down his face. He hadn't bothered to dress up, or even clean up, for this meeting. But that was okay. She hadn't either -- not that her office work made her dirty.

He showed her the print shop, which he had recently sold, and the other buildings. In each store or shop, he explained what their business goal was, who they hired to manage the operation and how business was going. Also, he was careful to point out the intricacies of the renovation work performed by Person's Fine Woodworking.

In the upper floors of one of the buildings was the latest project, still underway. Person and his colleagues were planning to market a new roofing process that they were developing. Through their years of experience, he and his workers had come up with some new ideas on how to make roofing material. Their roofing could be applied faster and at less cost while lasting much longer than conventional roofing materials. The project was still in development.

The renovation of the new business location had started,

but was abandoned as soon as the Benham contract was signed. Here Mitchell and Sandy stood, amongst stacks of lumber and building materials, while Person pointed out various plans.

Finally, talk ceased. Person walked over to the window, put his foot on the sill, crossed his arms on his raised knee, and looked out the window. Sandy sat on a stack of two-by-fours and watched him, admiring the man and the world he had built around him. It was quiet for a while.

Abruptly, he turned, walked to her, grabbed her and put his mouth against hers, pulling their bodies together with his lean, rugged arms. She submitted instantly, and responded with equal intensity and passion.

Much later, they rested, naked, in each others arms on the sawdust-covered floor. Sandy adjusted herself to get a better look at him, knocking a wood scrap out of the way to make room for her elbow.

"So, what are you after?"

"I think I just got it."

She grabbed another small wood scrap and dropped it on his head. "Funny. I mean, what are you trying to prove with all this? What's going on around here?"

"Profit. I'm after profit. My co-workers are after profit. Every business on this block and everyone who works here is after profit. We are fiercely devoted to our need and ability to create, but those creations become a stopping point if they don't also turn a profit. Profit from once creation let's us start the next one. Money, success, self-fulfillment. It's that easy."

"It may be that simple, but its not very popular."

"That depends on who you poll." He pushed up to a sitting position, still facing her. "Look, we went into this redevelopment thing because we believed there was profit to be had. We wanted to create commerce, and we wanted to do it for our own benefit. We planned to profit through a bigger bank account and our feeling of accomplishment by creating something that others could not or would not do."

"It looks like you were trying improve the plight of your fellow man," she replied, getting up to put on her clothes.

"Don't for a minute confuse our actions with some humanitarian aid project. All that 'reaching out to help the poor' crap doesn't work. The motivations are all wrong."

She stopped and glared at him. "Thanks for telling me my job is worthless. I bust my ass to help these people."

"Is it working? Do you launch people into instant prosperity? Or do you find yourself running into red tape, contradictory programs and confused goals which leave both you and your clients frustrated and depressed?"

She was quiet as she got up and put on her dusty clothes. She walked to the window to watch the neighborhood beyond Person's block. Youngsters who should have been in school were roaming the streets in packs. Windows on homes and apartments were boarded up. Trash and filth lay in the gutters. The neighborhood beyond this island of commerce was crumbling before her eyes.

He continued, "There is nothing wrong with helping someone if you do it because it will make both you and the person you help better off. But our government's system of aid to the poor dehumanizes the recipient.

"It's like we're telling them that their individual worth is so poor that we have to supplement it. Do we really have their best interests at heart when we put them in that position?

"While our government argues with itself about whether this benefit is a right, or whether that benefit is fair, or whether we need to increase or decrease this benefit, the poor feel more and more helpless. How would you feel if your income was determined by a bunch of arguing buffoons in the legislature?"

For an instant, a smile broke through her serious expression. But the solemn look returned and she didn't say anything, so he continued.

"Our country can't afford to keep poor people locked in these neighborhoods. We need strong minds and bodies, driven by their own selfish need to produce, create and chase profits. But these folks are trapped either by a lack of transportation to job areas or by ignorant racism that barricades them from their potential.

The drive for creativity and profit is everywhere, but when the legitimate channels are cut off, people turn to graffiti or illegal business to fulfill their needs. It's a waste.

"I came here for purely economic reasons. The property was affordable. My colleagues and I expanded into these other business ventures for the same reasons. We saw cheap capital and under-utilized labor that could bring us a profit. We did *not* start these businesses because we saw a neighborhood that needed help.

"All we had to do was find some people who shared our same selfish motivations. It took a lot of sorting out. Some of our neighbors have been poor, downtrodden and dependent on others for so long they did not have enough soul left to strive for personal excellence."

He realized he had been talking for a while, so he stopped to see her reaction. She looked depressed.

"Listen Sandy, when you left my shop last week, a couple of your former clients came up to me and told me about you. They said you were the only social worker they ever dealt with that treated them like men, like real members of society. They told me that if it hadn't been for you, they might have lost confidence in themselves and probably wouldn't be here today.

"I invited you back because I wanted you to see what I am doing and why. I thought you'd understand."

She did.

<u>ELEVEN</u>

The old man looked at Ron Davis with weary eyes. He was one of the men who had recruited Davis to the ACC those many years ago, and Davis rewarded the man by making sure he was in charge of recruiting for as long as he wanted it.

Today, he didn't want it very much because he had to report failure to Davis.

"No luck, huh?" Davis asked the man after he gave Davis the thumbs-down sign.

"My men have been casing Person's shops for the past few weeks, but we haven't found anybody who looked right," the recruiter told him.

Davis knew how his friend worked. The recruiter and his men would watch a company's employees to look for one who looked despondent or unhappy. They would keep an eye on that worker until they were pretty sure he was displeased with his job, not some other personal problem. Preferably, he would be a worker that the other employees either liked or respected. If he fit the profile, they would move in and steadily pitch the benefits of ACC solidarity.

They couldn't always find an ideal candidate, but they

were polished enough and experienced enough that they could usually make a successful move with a worker who didn't fit the perfect profile.

The recruiter continued, "All the workers looked overworked. I mean, they looked exhausted when they left the shops and job sites at the end of the day. But at the same time, they looked satisfied.

"I don't know how they could be happy. They work their asses off, but they don't earn union scale. Well it was frustrating enough that we took a chance."

Davis stared at him more intently. "What do you mean?"

"The more I thought about it, the more I figured maybe these guys just didn't know they weren't being paid the union rate. Maybe we could stir up some trouble. You know, these workers are all dumb Blacks from bad neighborhoods. I guessed we could get them rattled if we could make them feel that Person was taking advantage of them."

"And?"

"It didn't work. One day I sent our Black recruiter to talk to one of the guys who looked really beat. I mean, this guy was worn thin, but he had that wise-ass smile that all Person's guys have. It's like he's passing out drugs or something. You ought to check into that."

Davis smiled to himself. He sent his PI out to check out the personal side of Mitch Person. He was scheduled to talk to the PI after this meeting because there was some "urgent information." Maybe there was some drug stuff going on and they could sink Person in a heartbeat.

"Anyway," the recruiter continued, "this guy started laughing at my recruiter. Just laughing right in his face. Then he gets all serious, looks my guy right in the eye, and tells him to get his worthless ass out of Laughton Park. He says the ACC ain't got no business there and it ain't wanted."

"So you picked the wrong guy and moved too fast," Davis said in reprimanding tone.

"Listen Ron, I told you that Person's companies are too young. They ain't been around long enough for the workers to be really pissed off yet. But you wanted to push it so we picked the best guy available and it blew up in our face."

"And now Person will know what we are up to."

"That may not be all bad. If he overreacts and starts threatening his people about unions, it might backfire against him. Management gets panicky, starts cracking down on worker freedoms, and boom, the workers start coming to us in droves. It's worked before."

"We'll see," Davis replied. "In the mean time, keep an eye on those workers, but keep a low profile. Maybe pull some of our guys out of the area. We don't want to be too obvious."

"I already did that. We're cleared out but we're all set to pick up the pieces if something breaks."

Davis showed the man to his door, keeping a concerned frown on his face. The thing was, he admired this man and knew he was doing a good job. But Davis felt his men always performed better if they thought Davis was displeased. It made them work harder to please him, he believed. The arrogance of this thought was not evident to Ron Davis.

He went back to his desk and scribbled on some paperwork, waiting for the PI to show up.

The PI marched in without knocking, as usual, and plopped down in the chair across from Davis' desk. Davis was always just a little bit bothered that the PI wasn't more reverent. But he needed the sneaky bastard and, to tell the truth, was afraid to ever get on the bad side of the guy. Davis had seen enough of his work to believe that he already had a "Davis Blackmail" file in case the construction boss ever crossed him or fired him. Davis let the PI act however he pleased.

"For the most part, this guy leads a pretty dull life," he said. This time he held onto the file rather than hand it over immediately, as he usually did. Davis notice the difference, but didn't mention it. "He goes out for an occasional beer. No drugs. No perversions. No material excesses. No embezzlement. But about a week ago a female interest appeared on the scene."

Davis perked up with the report of a woman 's involvement. He extended his hand for the PI's folder.

As he handed it over he said, "I have some pictures of her. You may them find interesting. I haven't gotten any compromising photos yet that prove romantic activity, but it's pretty clear from their body language that they are very interested in each other."

He sat back with a smirk as Davis opened the folder.

The color drained from Davis' face. He sat silent for a while and out of the corner of his eye he could see the PI grinning at him, the asshole. Finally, he closed the folder and looked directly at his man.

"Thank you for the information. This is adequate for now. You do not need to follow them anymore or take any additional pictures."

"You're the boss," the detective said as he got up to leave.

Davis followed him to the door. "I'm sure I don't need to remind you to keep your findings confidential."

"It's part of my job. Don't worry about it."

After the PI left, he went back to his desk and opened the folder again. He was thankful that there were no graphic photos. He had seen some pretty raunchy photos from this detective, and they would have only added to the embarrassment of seeing his daughter as the subject of one of his own investigations.

It was time to give Sandy a call.

****

In the break room, the usual gang gathered to discuss business. The original five workers gathered there regularly to discuss developments and strategy.

Although the workers in all the Laughton Park businesses considered these five men the "management," no one felt uncomfortable around them. Person had a strict policy that all break room meetings were open to every employee. Even the newest employee was welcome to come to a meeting and give input on the decisions. Most of the time, only the five attended, but every now and then different employees would come and offer suggestions. Many times these suggestions were accepted, with credit going to the proper source.

This time a new face was the center of attention. Willie Bender was hired fairly recently by Person's Fine Woodworking, and, like most of his colleagues, was an excellent worker. He was finishing his story about being approached by an ACC recruiter.

"What'd you tell him?" asked Harry Tom.

"I told him to go to hell. I said the ACC wasn't welcome here or needed here," Bender replied.

"Thanks. I'm glad you think so," smiled Person.

"Well, it looks like we've finally been discovered," said Nate Elders. "I figured this Benham project would turn a few heads. Nobody knew us or cared about us until we grabbed a big project out from under them. Now Ron Davis and his cronies are trying to figure out who we are." He smiled and turned to Person. "I bet he shit his pants when he found out you used to work for him."

"You guys can laugh if you want to but it scares me," said Travis Niles. "The law firm I used to work for had some dealings with Ron Davis. That guy is a bad-ass. He doesn't piss around. If you cross him, he just looks for a way to rip your throat out and then he does it. No hesitation.

"If he's determined to bring the ACC in here then either he'll do it or he'll find some other way to cripple us."

Ramsey turned back to Bender. "What do you think Willie?"

Here he was, in front of his bosses, being asked to answer important questions. Yet Willie Bender felt comfortable. His managers weren't trying to put him on the spot or to criticize him. They were genuinely interested in his opinion. Before this job, no one ever asked him for his opinion or listened when he gave it. He loved his new job.

"I don't think anybody who works on this block would let an ACC member through the door," he said. "I ain't been here very long, but I've met all the other workers, and I ain't seen nobody even the least bit unhappy with their jobs. The ACC can't offer nothing to these people."

"Yeah, but they're ruthless," said Niles. "They keep looking and looking until they find some little crack, then they drive a wedge in and try to split the place apart. I think we better do something."

"I'm not so sure," Person said. "I think the other workers, like us, feel a part of this organization. We've all gotten where we are without the ACC, and we don't want them in here to claim credit for any of it or to try to take it away. Besides, a lot of the people here have been burned by the ACC at one time or another."

"I worked for ACC once before," Bender jumped in. "They protected the guys who didn't do anything and they made sure those same guys got as much money as I did. And the more years you sat on your ass the more money you made. I'm going back on unemployment before I work in an ACC shop again."

Person said, "I'm with Willie. Let them try to come in here. I don't think they can do it. But if they do, let them have it. I won't stick around. Willie won't stick around. I doubt if any of you would stick around. There is no company without the workers we have here now. This crew would be tough to replace."

"You built this operation from the ground up," Niles said.

"You mean to tell me you could just walk away from it? I don't believe you."

"Look, Travis, I'm in this business for two reasons. Because I love to build and because I want to earn money from my work. If the ACC starts running things, then they will take away my joy of building. Also, they will zap the profits. It would be better to me and my soul if I sold the place at whatever profit or loss I could make and go work where I can continue to enjoy my trade."

"But don't you see what you've done to this neighborhood? How could you turn your back on all these people you've helped?"

Person suddenly got very serious. "I have not driven one nail because I thought it would help someone else. I have done everything I have done for my own benefit. Our own individual selfishness is what has made this project work. Sure some other people have been helped by our efforts, but if for one minute we think we are working for them, if for one minute we lose our dedication to ourselves, then this will all be lost.

"If the ACC comes in here and tries to make me work for the benefit of my co-workers, then they will have taken the one driving force of our success. I would leave in an instant rather than let that happen."

The room was quiet for a while. Then Harry Tom started laughing.

"What's so damn funny," Elders asked.

"I just keep thinking about Ron Davis checking us out. You think he shit when he found out Mitch used to work for him, imagine what he did when he found out Mitch was dating his daughter."

The room burst out with laughter, except for Mitch Person. His jaw dropped and the color left his tanned face. Harry Tom caught the expression.

"You mean you didn't know?"

"My God, why didn't anybody tell me?"

"We all knew. We thought for sure you did too. Don't you ever talk to the women you date?"

"It never came up. I can't believe it."

Harry Tom started laughing again. "I bet Ron Davis' expression wasn't half as funny as yours was."

TWELVE

"Seth Howard is impressed with what you have done with the Laughton Park neighborhood. He would like to meet with you to discuss your techniques," the staffer told Person through the phone.

"Who's Seth Howard?" Person responded. He spent most of his life focusing on what he himself was doing. So he honestly did not know -- or care for that matter -- who Seth Howard was.

The response caught the staffer off guard. He was trained to handle all sorts of situations, but this was unexpected. How could this guy be a successful businessman and not know about Seth Howard? Despite the surprise answer, the staffer adjusted quickly and continued the conversation. If there was an awkward pause, it was imperceptible to the man on the other end of the phone.

"Representative Howard is a very powerful member of the state legislature. He represents the area where your business is located and he has been working to bring commerce and jobs to the area. In fact, he created the enterprise zone where you are located."

"And he wants to meet with me to talk about economic development?" Person pondered that for a second. "My experience has been that government is not very adept at forcing commerce and growth to take place. They always seem to be a step or two behind the entrepreneurs and industrialists. I don't see how we would have much to talk about."

"Actually, I think you have a lot in common. Representative Howard also believes that government is too bulky," the staffer lied. "He wants to figure out ways to provide incentives for business expansion while reducing government regulations at the same time."

The staffer let that sink in for a few seconds then added. "You have to admit the enterprise zone he created helped you get going."

"That's true." Person thought about that for a minute. The enterprise zone had been a big boost, although he had been amazed at all the paperwork and regulations that accompanied his tax break. Still, he should take at least a few minutes to show his gratitude to the man who made the tax break possible.

"Okay. A meeting would be fine."

"Fantastic. Representative Howard will be thrilled to hear this. How about the day after tomorrow at 1:30?"

Person looked at his calendar. A 1:30 appointment would allow him the morning to work at the Benham site. If the meeting was short he could go back and put in more time in the afternoon. "Um, yeah that should work."

"Great. We'll see you then," the staffer said with feigned excitement. "Oh. By the way. Representative Howard would like to bring along a reporter from the *Times-Union*. He feels the media should have a chance to see what you are doing. That okay?"

"Uh, yeah." Person's companies were enjoying a steady stream of business. But he figured a little positive publicity wouldn't hurt. "Oh! Will there be a photographer along?"

"Probably. Is that a problem."

"Well, I plan to work at a job site that morning so I will be wearing work clothes. Should I plan to clean up and change into a tie for the meeting?"

"I think that would be a good idea. It would make the photos look better."

"Okay. Thanks."

"We'll see you in two days. Bye."

After hanging up the phone, Person called in Travis Niles for advice. He trusted the former attorney's opinions on the local political scene.

"I'm meeting with a Representative Seth Howard in two days, but I don't know who he is," Person explained.

"Jeez Mitch, you really need to get out more. Seth Howard is the most powerful man in state politics. He could screw you from both directions and look good doing it," said Niles.

"Why does he want to see you. I'm a little nervous," he added.

"His staff person said he is impressed with our commerce project and wants to discuss how he can make government be more helpful and less burdensome to business."

"He said that?" Niles thought for a minute. "Mitch, this sounds like bad news. Howard is an asshole. He may talk a good line, but he strongly believes that government is the savior of the people, or at least the savior of his own career. I can't believe he is at all interested in reducing government influence. If he is, it would be the first time."

"What do you think?"

"Is the media involved in your meeting?"

"A reporter from the *Times-Union*. Why?"

"I think he is going to come here to take credit for all these new jobs and then find a way to shut you down as soon as the ink dries on the *Times-Union* pages."

"I don't see what he can do. All these companies are pretty healthy. Even if he dismantles the enterprise zone, each of these companies could find a way to handle the higher tax burden."

"That's just it with Seth Howard. He always finds a way that you wouldn't expect. You can't anticipate his next move and you better not underestimate him. Do you want me to stick around during the meeting to see if I can figure out what he's up to?"

"I don't know. It's bad enough that I'm going to be away from the Benham site for part of an afternoon. I would hate for two of us to be missing..."

"Don't be short-sighted about this Mitch. None of us will be able to work on the Benham site if Howard decides to screw us before its complete. Better for two men to miss one afternoon than for the project to be taken away from us completely."

"I suppose you're right. I'd appreciate your being here. Thanks for the offer."

"No problem, Mitch. It'll make me feel better too."

"Great. Wear a tie. We want your old attorney buddies to see you looking good in the newspaper."

"Christ. I was hoping when I left that I'd never have to wear another tie. I haven't thrown 'em away yet, though, so I might as well get some use out of them."

"Speaking of...I don't think I even have a tie. Suppose I could borrow one of yours?"

"Good idea," Niles laughed. "In fact, I've seen the way you dress. You might want me to pick out your outfit for you. Better yet, maybe Sandy could borrow some of her dad's clothes for you."

Person laughed. He had been the butt of jokes about his relationship all day and was taking it well. Inside, however, his stomach knotted up. He hadn't called Sandy yet and wasn't sure he would know exactly what he would say to her. He was not looking forward to their next conversation, but he planned to call her that evening after work.

****

He was on his way over. Sandy was nervous. Mitch called and said he just found out who her dad was.

The phone conversation had not gone well. She laughed at first because she thought he knew all along, and the mental image of the look on his face when he discovered her lineage was hilarious. Then he said people had been laughing at him all day, and she felt bad for him.

He was obviously upset, so she suggested he come over so they could talk about it face to face.

She was preparing some coffee when the doorbell rang.

"Hi Mitch. Come on in."

He perched on the edge of the sofa in the living room of her small, modestly furnished apartment while she went to the kitchen to pour the coffee.

"Well, how are you doing?" she called in to him.

"Not bad really. The shock has finally subsided."

"I'm sorry I laughed."

"That's all right. I'm used to it thanks to my caring colleagues."

"It's just that we have been seeing each other nearly every day for over two weeks. We talk enough about the construction business that I was sure you knew why I was familiar with it. And it's not like I have a different name." She came back into the room carrying the drinks.

"There are probably a zillion Davises in the phone book that aren't related to Ron." (He thought about, but didn't add, "and probably a hundred other children who are related but don't share his last name.") "I just didn't make the connection. Now that I look back it's kind of obvious."

She watched him for a while. He was struggling with something he wanted to tell her or ask her. She waited patiently.

Finally, he blurted, "Are you like him? Do you think like him? I've got to know."

Now she was angry. "Goddamn you! How can you ask such a question. We've spent so much time talking. Didn't you ever listen to me? Don't you know me at all?"

He was sinking into the sofa. Unfortunately, not far enough to hide from her rage.

She didn't let up. "You of all people should know people have to judge other people on their own merits, not their race, gender, clothes, makeup or family background. Why should I be judged any differently? Why did your rules change all of a sudden?

She paused for a minute and turned inward. He knew better than to say anything.

"How could you be so weak?" She raced to the door and opened it. "Get out," she said coolly.

He slinked out of the apartment, down the stairs and into the night.

She collapsed into her sofa and turned on the TV, hoping it would work its usual mind-numbing magic. She would not cry. It was not something she did for anyone. But she was upset...and disappointed.

Other men had left because of her father, but it was usually because they were afraid of him or because he did something to scare them off. No one had ever left before because he was afraid of her dad's philosophy. That's because no one had for one second thought she might be anything like her dad.

Now that she had finally met a man who could tell there

was something wrong with Ron Davis' way of thinking, the man could not see that she and her father were very, very different. This disappointed her.

She had fallen asleep on the sofa, thanks to another inane sitcom, when the doorbell woke her.

She opened the door, and without a greeting Person started talking, "You know, I could probably get along with your father. I could sit in a room with him and chat, smoke cigars, drink beer and watch football. I wouldn't agree with anything he said, but I could get along with him because I accept him as he is.

"He stands for everything that is wrong with many people. To me, he is a symbol of the wall against which I must continually push. Yet, I accept him as he is because I've learned that it's never worth the effort to hate anyone or anything.

"With that simple philosophy, I can tolerate anyone. I practically worship the people I know who believe in themselves. Those people stand as a symbol of everything I am. They are the ones with whom I feel a friendship, no, a kinship.

"But most people are insecure. They waste themselves on envy, or a quest for power over others or some other misuse of their real abilities. I meet people like that every day, but I don't try to change them. Really, I don't waste a thought on them."

She finally butted in, "Where are you going with this?"

"I can't understand why I suddenly started worrying about your beliefs. Why didn't I just casually accept anything you might have turned out to be? It's easy for me to understand your father. It's apparent you don't think like him, so why was I scared that you might have some hidden resemblance?"

She thought for a moment. "Maybe you need me more than you do other people." While this would seem like a pretty obvious answer to most people, she knew it was a big jump for him to take.

"I've been walking the streets like the star of some bad movie trying to figure this out. I'm fiercely devoted to myself and letting others be themselves. I don't expect things from other people. I consider that an invasion of their privacy. I appreciate when people act in accordance with my beliefs, but I don't try to change those who can't.

"But you are different. I care what you think. I actually care what you think of me too. You and I have crossed that threshold from individualism to sharing. I consider that threshold sacred.

"I can't believe I almost blew it. I didn't see what was going on. I'm sorry."

They looked at each other for awhile. Suddenly she realized that they had not moved since she opened the door. She invited him in.

In a short time, their clothes were on the floor and their bodies were on the worn sofa. Intertwined, they reveled in their passion for each other. Their lovemaking was the physical symbol of each releasing his and her soul to the other. Their closely guarded individuality was given up for the benefit of the other and only the other.

THIRTEEN

Representative Seth Howard was due to arrive any minute. Person supposed he should be nervous, but he was not. Sandy had added her warnings to Travis', and now Travis Niles was pacing the floor in Person's office mumbling to himself. Yet, both outwardly and inwardly, Person was calm. After all, what could this politician do to him?

When the lawmaker arrived, staffer, reporter and photographer in tow, Person rose to greet him. The man did not fit the image Person had formed after listening to Travis and Sandy. Howard was not a large ogre with blood dripping from sharp fangs. Rather, he was below average in height and he was slight of build, excepting the paunch hanging over his belt. Furthermore, he did not possess the good looks characteristic of most successful politicians. He was a few years older than Person. Overall, he was sort of small and plain-looking, almost homely. Nice suit though.

"Mitchell Person? Seth Howard," said the man, extending his hand. "Pleased to finally meet you."

"Thank you sir."

"Oh, please call me Seth. And you are?" he asked approaching Niles. Introductions were made all around the room and a few minutes of small talk ensued.

Person could now see how the man had gotten to his position. He was just as comfortable as Person, even in these totally foreign surroundings with two other men he was meeting for the first time. Howard was disarming. He had apparently trained himself to ease into control of whatever situation he was in. Person noticed that he had somehow maneuvered himself to a position where everyone in the room would be facing him at all times. Person figured this was a skill polished with years of experience. It was second nature, done without a thought.

The *Times-Union* reporter was Aaron Teldon. Bearded, somewhat scruffy and dressed out of style, Teldon looked the part of a man ready to fight the big-business establishment at a moment's notice. He had not outgrown the misplaced idealism of his college years. His eyes darted continuously about the room, missing nothing. His photographer was dressed worse and looked bored, casually snapping a picture or two of the shop and the people in it.

Person glanced at Niles and caught his attention. He could tell the former attorney did not like the looks of Teldon. Niles shot back a look of concern.

Howard's staffer was a clean-shaven, professionally dressed man in his early twenties who looked even younger. He also carried a camera. Later, Niles explained to Person that the staffer took pictures to be used in newsletters and campaign brochures.

"Well Mitchell, how about giving us a brief tour of your

little empire here. Explain how you've created this remarkable renovation," said the lawmaker.

Niles noticed that the politician was not committing to either approval or disapproval yet. Because he used words like "little empire" and "remarkable" rather than "accomplishment" and "fantastic," his comments could be read as either praise or condemnation, depending on the public's reaction to Person. If the man was impressed or outraged, it did not show.

Person showed the men around his workshop, which was mostly empty because the workers were out at various job sites, and a few of the other enterprises on the block. As they strolled back to Person's Fine Woodworking, he began to explain the management philosophy behind the production.

"Each of these companies relies heavily on the labor, the men and women who are committed to their jobs. Because of that, we can't run these operations the same way we would run machines. Instead, we have to keep an open management system where each worker is able to have input into management decisions."

Aaron Teldon had been scribbling notes through the whole tour and was now ready to start asking questions. "How often do they actually make management decisions?"

"Really not that often. We have a small committee of me, Mr. Niles here and a few more of the original employees of Person's Fine Woodworking. We meet regularly to discuss the operations of each business. Our meetings are open to the other employees but we don't require them to attend. We figure that they will come to us if they have anything to add. Sometimes the newer employees will attend just to see what the meetings are like.

Other times, people will offer good suggestions that we quickly adopt. But most of the time, the employees trust us to make the right decision. They have worked hard all day and would rather rest at home than stay late to attend a business meeting."

Sensing danger, Niles added, "I think every worker feels welcome. They don't feel shut out of the process at all."

Teldon jumped to the next topic. "You said your companies rely heavily on your workers, but I understand that you won't let your workers unionize." Someone from Howard's staff had fed the reporter background information ahead of time.

"It's not a question of letting them unionize. I don't have that kind of control over anybody. It's more a situation of them not wanting a union. To tell the truth, I don't see how a union would fit in here," answered Person honestly.

Niles was beginning to get nervous. To him, this looked like a set up and Person was walking right into it. He wished his boss would talk in circles or polish his responses the way a politician does. But he knew Person either could not or would not pull punches. His boss had a complete indifference toward others' opinions of him, so he saw no need to sugar-coat anything he said. So far, there were no serious problems, but Niles felt pretty certain things were not going their way. If only he knew exactly where the big blow would come from.

The reporter continued. "For one, your workers are paid below union scale aren't they?"

"That's true. It's what helps us stay competitive. Our work is far better than anybody else in town. That's why we get most of our clients, but we have to offer a competitive price too."

"You think that's fair that they work hard but aren't paid as much as they might be somewhere else?"

"Well, I have never heard a complaint about salary yet. I think most of these people would work for half of what they are earning now just for the opportunity to work where they are respected as individuals and craftsmen. Besides, they are free to leave if they feel they are treated unfairly. There are other companies in town."

Person was still nonplussed. He was receiving a good grilling but didn't look under the gun at all. Howard and his staffer were impressed with Person's cool under pressure. Howard could handle media scrutiny with ease, but most business-types quickly became defensive and gave terrible interviews when the pressure increased. Person, however, didn't view the interview as a grilling. To him it was an honest exchange of views and opinions.

"But a union could offer them a sense of security..."

Person cut him off. "A union would strip them of their individuality. These men and women are good because they are motivated by their own self interests and are guided by their own talents. They are content here because they are allowed to use their skills as they see fit. There is no duty to a group or solidarity or anything else to hold them back. If these were union shops then every worker would have his and her duties assigned to them. Every assignment is a limit.

"Sure, they must work together," he continued. "But they work together out of a sense of a respect for one another. They divide tasks and share responsibilities in an effort to complete the final project. There is no squabbling over clean-up being someone else's job, or quality control being the duty of the supervisor. Everybody does everything that must be done and they do it well."

"That doesn't seem very efficient," Teldon remarked.

"It would only be inefficient if the workers did not feel a part of the project. But they know what the project is and what must be done to complete it. The division of tasks is an automatic thing that just happens. Each of these workers is skilled and proud. That is all they need in order to be efficient. What would really bog things down is if I sat down each morning and tried to figure out what each man and woman should do that day. How can I anticipate every action of every person at a job site? I can't, so I don't try.

"If the ACC stuck its nose in here, then we would have to have one crew in to saw boards and another crew in to run wires and another one in to hang windows and so on. God forbid if one of the electricians needed a hole in a floor joist to make room for some conduit. He couldn't just grab a drill and do it, he would have to get the foreman of the hole drillers to assign someone to do it for him. Now *that's* inefficiency."

Niles noticed that the reporter looked bored with Person's rambling. Howard and his staffer were glazed over as well. And the photographer was starting to put away his equipment.

Teldon flipped through his notebook and acted like he was just planning to check for accuracy of a few comments. Niles didn't buy the act and was bracing himself for the Big Question.

"Mr. Person, I've noticed that, with the exception of you and Mr. Niles, every worker I've seen today is Black. Is that right?"

Niles thought, "Come on Mitch. Start lying. Make up something. Don't be so damned honest about this one." But he didn't say anything out loud, or even try to signal Person, because he knew it wouldn't affect his boss.

Person answered, "Yes. With the exception of two other men on the management committee, every other employee is Black. These urban neighborhoods are filled with untapped resources. Strong, bright men and women are trapped here. Many of them have not had an opportunity to find jobs where they are treated as individuals. We looked for the best. We found them. And we have all benefited because of it."

"Haven't you merely taken advantage of their situation to get low-priced workers? You say they are free to leave, but can they really? Do they have access to transportation? It seems as if you have found cheap labor and are hiding it under the shroud of a charitable project in the inner city," the reporter said.

"No. This is not a charitable project. Not at all," said Person.

Niles looked to the heavens. "Please shut up, Mitch," he thought. But he knew this was Person's favorite topic and there would be no stopping him.

Person continued. "I started my business and expanded to these other operations to help myself. I did it for my own benefit. I decided to locate here because I could afford it, and I decided to stay because it is where my profit margin is the highest. If no one else will hire the talented African-American men and women in this neighborhood, then I will. Not because I feel sorry for them, but because they will help me be successful. Selfishness is the only sincere charity."

Howard's jaw dropped. He had never seen someone commit suicide before, and he figured this would be the closest he would ever come. It was fascinating. Although he was impressed with the revitalization of Laughton Park, he was glad he had not embraced the man who made it possible.

Teldon scribbled furiously. Finally, he stopped and asked, "The one business you already sold to the Black manager, how much profit did you make on that deal?"

"I'm not comfortable giving you an exact figure, but it was satisfactory."

"It wasn't just Mitch who made these decisions. The entire committee was in on them because we all have money invested in these companies," said Niles. He was determined not to let Person take the fall alone. The amazing thing to him was that Person still seemed completely calm. Couldn't he tell what was happening?

Closing his notebook, the reporter said he was out of questions. Howard, the staffer and Teldon walked back to Howard's car. The news photographer had his equipment back out and was shooting furiously. Howard started directing his staffer to take certain pictures. The reporter re-opened his notebook and started talking to Howard.

When Person and Niles got back inside, Person said, "I think that went okay."

Niles stopped in his tracks and screamed, "You have got to be kidding. They opened the trap door and you walked right in."

Person looked confused. "I thought we had a civil

exchange of ideas. I thought I made a pretty good case."

"Like I said before, you need to get out more." Niles calmed down. He didn't like yelling at Mitch when the man was merely being naive. Mitch's innocence and his devotion to his ideal were appealing. It only became annoying when they were confronted with the powers that make things work in the real world. "You need to understand that the glory of selfishness doesn't play well in the media."

"But I'm not going to change what I believe just to appease some reporters and politicians."

"I know that. That's why I didn't try to stop you. But listen, I think they are really going to play up this Black-worker thing. It will be pretty easy to make it look like you took advantage of the neighbors to make a profit."

"I'm proud of our profits, but I didn't take advantage of anyone. It would be a waste of time to take advantage of someone. That would be the same as letting someone else dictate your actions, because you would be dependent on them for your achievements..."

"You're preaching to the choir." Niles looked exhausted. "You asked me to come along and give you my perspective. I'm just saying that they are going to kick your ass in the paper tomorrow. Don't be surprised. You live and die by your philosophy. You may have your chance to prove your devotion."

"Thanks, Travis. I appreciate your insight."

The two men parted and Person went into his office and closed the door. Shortly, the phone rang.

"How did it go?" Sandy asked.

"I thought it went fine, but Travis thinks they are going to rip out my liver and serve it to the vultures."

"I trust Travis' opinion on this one."

"Yeah, you may be right. Want some company tonight?"

"Sure, but aren't you worried about what's going to happen?"

"Not really. What happens happens. I've never been concerned about other people's opinions of me, yourself excepted of course. I'm not about to start basing my actions on how I think it will play out in the paper."

"Unfortunately, public opinion can have a big impact on your opportunities for business."

"I'd rather starve than succumb."

FOURTEEN

Local developer creating slave empire?

by Aaron Teldon

Washington City -- A local businessman has stirred a controversy over an urban renovation project that critics say resembles a return to the days of slavery.

Mitchell Person used enterprise zone tax breaks to start a string of businesses in the blighted Laughton Park area of the city. The businesses have enjoyed remarkable success in a short period of time, but critics charge that the profits are the result of a mistreated workforce rather than Person's business acumen.

"While I'm pleased to see new jobs in our urban areas, I'm severely disturbed with the way these jobs were created," said state Representative Seth Howard, a Washington City legislator.

"It appears as if a few white investors are getting rich by under-paying their African-American employees. This seems reminiscent of the days of slavery," he added.

Person acknowledged that his African-American workforce is paid below the union scale. He said the reduced salaries help his companies stay competitive, but he also said his motivations were for profit, rather than the well-being of those employees.

"I started my business and expanded to these other operations to help myself. I did it for my own benefit. If no one else will hire the talented African-American men and women in this neighborhood, then I will. Not because I feel sorry for them, but because they will help me be successful," Person said.

Person founded Person's Fine Woodworking five years ago with three other white employees. Those men pooled their money to start other new companies in the Laughton Park neighborhood. Person said their plan is to sell the newer companies to each company's African-American executive manager at a profit. This has already happened with the first satellite business they launched.

Local African-American leaders said they knew about the revitalization in their neighborhood, but they were unaware of the motives behind the renovation project.

"This is a tragedy. Our fine African-American men and women are being used to put fine suits on the backs of white industrialists," said Rev. Benjamin Walker, head of the Washington City Act Now organization. "Once again, the needs of the African-American man has not been taken into account."   look into the tax break

Howard said he would   status   of   Person's
                                             companies.

****

"I especially like the photograph," said Harry Tom. The gang was gathered in the break room going over the day's plans and discussing the *Times-Union* article. "How did that guy capture you and Travis in those fine suites standing next to Rudy Jefferson looking his worst? You two look like a couple of plantation owners."

"Rudy was doing his regular maintenance schedule on his equipment that day -- you know how he won't let anyone else work on his printers -- so he was an absolute mess. Well, he saw us walking by and came out to say hi. The photographer just snapped away," Person explained. "The funny thing is, I had to borrow that suit and tie from Travis."

For a few minutes, they chuckled over the ludicrous image painted by the photograph and article. However, Nate Elders wasn't saying much. Person noticed the silence.

"Nate, what do you think about this?"

The man sat there for a minute without saying anything. The laughter stopped and the room got quiet. Finally, he began to speak softly.

"Mitch, I know you judge a man based on what he is, not what he looks like, who he knows or who his friends are. I know you have given me and all the workers in these companies a chance to do what we want to do and be proud of it. I also know why you pay below union scale. You are a good man, and I think all the brothers who work here know it.

"The problem is that not all the brothers work here. Think of all the people we turned away, that we didn't hire. We didn't bring anyone on board unless we were confident that they were as self-reliant as we are. We wanted people who would work because they were proud, self-assured, and loved to create work in their own image. To build for building's sake. But you see Mitch, problems don't come from people who agree with you.

"These companies are a symbol of the human spirit. But that is a strange concept to most people. They will never understand. Most of us grew up thinking labor and management were separate. We have been taught that management is made up of rich tyrants while labor is made up of the struggling, hard-working poor.

"In reality, it doesn't work that way. The business owners are the ones who have a drive, a vision. They are the ones that take risks and struggle to make their company successful. Labor sits back, demands a regular paycheck, with regular raises, and doesn't care about the vision or the company. It's stupid, but they don't see the connection between that vision and their paychecks. Maybe it's because their risk is not as great. If the company is driven out of business, the employees have lost a paycheck, but the owner has lost his vision, a bit of his soul.

"When it becomes an issue of race, the real issues get

even more cloudy. If someone charges you with racism, it's easy for my brothers and me to believe it. That's because racism confronts us everywhere. If someone charges racism, they are usually right.

"Mitch, I know you consider racism inefficient. It's a waste of resources to worry about someone's skin color. But I know you think that way because I work with you and I know you. Other people will hear you are running a slave shop and will believe every word.

"It's your word against Benjamin Walker and Seth Howard. Who do you think people will believe? Will they believe the rich white guy who owns the businesses, or will they believe the Black civil rights leader and the liberal legislator?

"The vicious irony is that I can't get out there and try to defend you. Neither can the other brothers who work here and feel the same way you do. The minute I take your side I will be labeled a "Tom" or a mouthpiece. The brothers will stop listening.

"That's what you face Mitch. You better take it seriously because it didn't end with this article in the paper. It's just starting."

The men sat back and thought about what Elders told them. The silence was broken by the ringing of Mitch Person's phone.

"Hi Mitch, this is Tom Benham. I saw that piece of shit in the paper this morning, and I wanted to call and let you know I support you. You're a good man and you are doing an outstanding job with our project here at Benham United."

"Thanks, Tom. I appreciate the vote of confidence."

"Great. But listen. My public relations guy isn't as easy about this as I am. He is concerned about our company's image in light of this. He wanted me to check on your timetable and see when you are planning to be finished."

Person was stunned. Why should one article make any difference about this job? Shouldn't the quality of the work speak for itself? "Uh, within two weeks."

"That's fantastic. And any sooner would be better. Listen Mitch, I know what kind of man you are, but some of these weak-minded people I keep around here don't get it and they are going to start pushing me to keep our image clean. Don't worry because it's too late to back out on our contract, and I think your crew is doing the best work I have ever seen."

"Yes Tom. They're a great bunch of men and women. I'll pass along the praise to them."

"Good." Neither man said anything for a moment, then Benham added, "You may be in for a rough ride for a while. Let me know if there is something I can do."

"Thanks...You know, there may be something you can do. You know what you were saying about the quality of work, that it's the best you've seen? Would you mind telling the crew personally? They know they are the best, but in light of what may be coming, it could help them to hear it directly from their biggest client."

"Consider it done, Mitch. A bunch of them are already here this morning. I'll go talk to them now."

Back in the break room, Person announced to the others that they needed to extend work hours for the Benham project to try to complete it early. The other men understood the implicit message. The mood was somber as they re-worked the schedule.

****

"You did it again, Seth. I don't know how you come up with this stuff, but it works." Ron Davis had driven to the Statehouse that morning to meet with his legislative friend. When he read the morning paper at his breakfast table, he let out a loud whoop. Controlling himself, he sat back, relaxed, and smiled really big. He knew this was going to be a great day.

Howard sat in his office and quietly accepted the praise from Davis. To be honest, Howard didn't know how his visit to Laughton Park would turn out, until Person started laying on the profit and selfishness crap. In fact, many of Howard's greatest maneuvers were pulled off without a detailed plan. That didn't stop Howard from taking full credit for their success, however.

He was a shrewd politician. But despite how much planning and organization a person uses, political success still relies a great deal on being in the right place at the right time and knowing how to capitalize on changing situations.

How many bright, young people who would make outstanding leaders never had an opportunity to serve because they were too young when the voters wanted stately, experienced lawmakers? Then they were too old when voter favor switched toward younger, promising prospects. And how many intelligent, well-organized policy makers lost power when the someone else reacted more quickly to the changing headlines.

Howard had excellent instincts and fully understood their value. He didn't know exactly what would happen when he visited Laughton Park, but he knew he would be able to react to whatever did happen, and make himself look good. With Howard, the chance for glory was always greater than the risk.

One other important move that Howard learned was to never let on to someone that you didn't have the outcome planned to the letter. When things worked out, Howard always received credit for brilliant maneuvering. It was to his advantage to maintain this image. It helped generate fearful respect among his colleagues and associates.

"So what's our next move?" asked Davis.

"Right now, the staff is drafting legislation requiring any company receiving enterprise zone tax credits to pay the prevailing wage. I'm going to give Ben Walker a chance to stir some shit for a few days. Then I'll take my bill draft down to Laughton Park and hold a news conference."

Davis let out a sinister laugh, the way high school kids laugh when they just got away with toilet-papering the principal's house. "Do you think the bill will carry?" he asked.

"It really depends on how big of an issue this becomes. If we can paint this guy as a real slave-driving opportunist, it will be hard for anyone to come out on his side. The few hard-core, pro-business assholes will fight us, but we only need a majority to make it fly."

"What should I be doing?"

"Nothing right now. But be on the ready. I may call you as things heat up. And you may start setting aside some PAC money. I'm going to work on a list of people who will need some donations to be swayed to our side. The legislature starts up again in a couple of months and I'd like to have some firm support for this bill before I introduce it."

The two men exchanged small talk for a while. When the subject turned to Davis' family, the construction boss felt his stomach knot up. He hadn't yet called his daughter about her new boyfriend. He wanted to blame procrastination, but he knew that wasn't the real culprit. He was afraid of his daughter. She wouldn't try to hurt him physically or emotionally, but she wouldn't warm up to him either.

They got along just fine, but their relationship didn't go beyond the necessary action that went along with being related. Davis and his sons were regular pals, sharing stories, laughs and plans. But Sandy was different. Although he didn't understand what drove her or what she was thinking, he got the feeling she knew exactly what made him tick, probably better than he did. That one-sidedness to their relationship made him uncomfortable.

He enjoyed seeing her and talking with her during holidays and other times the family got together, and he wouldn't hesitate to call her if he found a nice young man for her to date, but he felt odd contacting her for other reasons. It was like entering a different world, one where he was not in control of everything.

He was sure she read the paper. He knew this was a good opportunity to call her.

FIFTEEN

When he got the phone call from the *Times-Union* reporter, Rev. Benjamin Walker was angry. If there was something wrong with the Laughton Park development, why didn't anyone tell him? In fact, he had been making preliminary plans to visit Mitchell Person himself. It would have been a great opportunity to bring the media out to photograph Rev. Walker shaking hands with a man who was giving good jobs to urban African-Americans.

Reading the paper this morning, Walker was thankful he hadn't moved with his plans yet. He was even more angry now than he was yesterday, though, because he had nearly walked into an embarrassing trap.

Why hadn't Seth Howard called him and let him know what was going on? He knew how that man planned. This thing didn't happen by accident. "I suppose now he's waiting for me to take over for a while," he thought out loud.

Walker and Howard worked together well. Although neither man trusted the other, they respected each other, and they frequently shared the same goals and they worked for a lot of the same constituency. Walker suspected that Howard kept him out of the loop on Laughton Park because he didn't want Walker to jump the gun and grab the media before Howard had the chance.

A few years ago, Walker had done just that. He and Howard were working on introducing a legislative program to help the inner-city poor. Once Walker had enough information about the program to know what he was talking about, he held a news conference to announce it. He gave Howard credit during the conference, but he had not invited the lawmaker, and all the headlines and editorials glorified Walker.

Howard never said anything to Walker about it, but the African-American leader noticed that he was kept out of the action from that point on. Throughout the legislative session, Howard held numerous news conferences to explain new developments and successes with the urban-aid package. Walker was never invited to any of them. The credit and praise for the program shifted from Walker to Howard. He got the message and never crossed Howard again. But the lawmaker had a long memory, so every now and then he would screw Walker again. Walker figured Laughton Park was another lesson from the Statehouse power-broker.

Now it was time to turn his attention away from his power struggles with Seth Howard and focus on a new power struggle with another man. He would have liked to have the time to check some facts and find out what exactly was going on in that renovated city block. Unfortunately, time was one thing he did not have. He needed to get TV cameras out to Laughton Park early that afternoon.

Many of his followers would be alarmed when they heard about a White man, in their neighborhood, getting rich by paying their brothers less money. But like Walker, most of them would not do anything based on what Seth Howard said. They would wait to hear from Ben Walker. They would follow his lead.

First, Walker made a call to start the phone tree that would gather a crowd by 1:00 that afternoon. Second, he started calling the media. He would work on fine-tuning his message later.

****

Rev. Walker and his troupe were milling about in front of Person's Fine Woodworking at 12:50 p.m. Some of them hadn't seen other members of the group for a while, so there was some chit-chat and catching-up to do. The atmosphere was relaxed until the first TV truck showed up.

As the reporter got out and the camera man began to set up his equipment, Walker went over to talk with them and explain the agenda, the best camera angle, etc. The group started to wander to their assigned positions. The frivolity had died down, but they were still holding personal conversations and discussing the Washington City football team. They were getting their signs ready and waiting for the signal from their leader.

Once the three network stations and Aaron Teldon were present, Walker decided it was time to start. There was an independent TV station in town, but they were always late and their viewership was too small to hold up this news conference. Besides, there were a couple other newspaper reporters and one radio reporter on hand. Walker had taken the time to personally say hello to each one of them.

As he walked toward the podium his helpers had placed, it was if someone had thrown a switch to turn on the crowd. They started chanting, yelling, waving signs and, in general, looking angry.

The podium and crowd were positioned so the cameras would capture Walker and his following making their statements right below the sign reading "Person's Fine Woodworking." All the crowd members were instructed to look clean and presentable, conservative styles. Walker didn't want them to look like an unruly mob, just a group of well-meaning but oppressed citizens. He was anticipating a good shot on the TV screen.

Like many civil rights leaders, Walker was a fantastic orator. He could read the directions off a packet of instant oatmeal and make it sound like the most important message anyone had ever heard. Act Now had been successful in bringing needed civil rights changes to Washington City in part because people liked to listen to Walker speak. His message was rarely forgotten by people who heard him.

His crowd quieted down to let him begin. They had been with him long enough that they were used to his rhythm of speaking. They instinctively knew when they were supposed to yell, chant, sing, or whatever it took to highlight his speech.

Because this was for the media, not a regular speech,

Walker knew he had to keep it short.

"How long must we wait?" he began.

"What have we asked of society but to be given the chance to be equal, productive members? We just want a chance to work, to pray and to raise a family as regular, equal members of society. How long must we wait?!" A few crowd members voiced their approval of his words.

"Our laws say you can't hold a man as a slave. Our laws say you can't pay a man less money for his work just because of the color of his skin. Our laws say you can't discriminate. We follow the laws and we are waiting for the laws to be followed for us. How long must we wait?!" The crowd broke out into a loud cheer. Walker figured this would be the sound bite of the night, but he needed to go on a little longer.

"Today, we see a man who comes to our neighborhood pretending to be a savior. He offers jobs to some of the poor. But does he come here to help? No, he comes here for greed, for profit, for a chance to get rich from the sweat of African-American men and women. How long must we wait?!" More cheering.

"We are peaceful, but we are also impatient. We are angry, but we are also sad. We are yelling for equality, but we are also crying from the lack of it. We are full of despair, but we are also driven by the light of hope." Long quiet pause.

"How long must we wait?!" The crowd erupted in cheering and chanting. Walker stepped away from the podium and toward the reporters to answer questions. His troops would continue to parade around in front of the building waving signs and chanting slogans. It would make a good backdrop for TV interviews.

****

Person was smoothing the joint compound on one of the new office walls at Benham United. Drywall work was a real art. Like an artistic painter uses different kinds of brushes to achieve the right effect, a drywall worker used different sized trowels to fill nail holes and the seams between sheets until the wall is perfectly smooth.

It is not an easy job to do correctly. Person was not good at it when he started his business. Fortunately, one of the men he hired from Laughton Park was masterful with a bucket of drywall mud, a roll of seam tape and an assortment of trowels. Person begged the man to give him lessons until Person felt comfortable doing a room on his own. The drywall expert still worked for Person's Fine Woodworking, so Person knew advice and help was always close at hand, though Person himself had become quite accomplished at the skill.

Finishing the drywall work right away was important so the mud could dry and be sanded in time for the painters to finish up. Person's Fine Woodworking had subcontracted the painting job to the Laughton Park painting company, which was called True Colors Painting. Person and his investors owned the company but the name was chosen by executive manager LaRon Dempsey. Like Rudy Jefferson with his print shop, Dempsey wanted a name for the painting company that hinted at its African-American management. Aside from displaying pride for his heritage, Dempsey hoped the name would give them a subtle advantage when minority hiring was a consideration.

Although Person still owned the painting company (he planned to sell it to Dempsey, at a profit, in about a year), he did not automatically award the subcontract to them. As with other projects where he needed to subcontract part of the work, he required his own companies to bid against any other firm that wanted the work. Neither he nor his investors were willing to hire their own firm for a Person's Fine Woodworking project if the company did not offer them a competitive deal and the best possible quality.

Sure, they could have made an automatic profit for their other companies if they always hired them, but they felt it would be more beneficial for the long-run health of those companies to make them earn every bid they won. In addition, Person and friends still needed to consider the reputation of Person's Fine Woodworking. They were not about to subcontract with a company, even one of their own, if that company could not meet their standards.

Not surprisingly, though, none of Person's other companies ever lost a bid to subcontract with Person's Fine Woodworking. They always bid a superior product at a competitive price. Those companies didn't always win their bids for other projects, but not every prospective client was looking for the same things Person demanded.

Person was just finishing the mud job when his cellular phone rang. He had a love-hate relationship with that phone. He hated the thought that while he had it with him, someone could always interrupt his work with a mere phone call. On the other hand, since he needed to be in touch with people by phone, he loved the fact that he did not have to be chained to a desk making or waiting on calls. He could still get out and create.

"Hello."

"Mitch. It's Rudy. You've got problems." Instantly, Mitch knew it was serious. His business neighbor had never called before. Even when Person was still the owner of the print shop, Rudy would not call if he had a question or problem. He was one of those people who usually made the correct decision, and if he was stumped, he wanted to try to find the answer himself before turning to someone else. He would usually wait until Person got back. Now that Rudy owned the shop, he had no reason to talk to Person about business problems, unless the two were cordially shooting the breeze and exchanging ideas.

"What's up?"

"We got about thirty brothers standing in front of your shop hollering and waving signs. And the TV guys are here covering the whole thing."

"Who the hell are they?"

"Rev. Walker is leading the pack, so they must be his boys. Damn them. They're raising all this shit and there ain't but a couple of those brothers even live in this neighborhood."

"What am I supposed to do?"

"I don't know about this shit, Mitch. Whatever you do, good luck."

Person thanked Jefferson for the call and walked through the job site looking for somebody to talk with. He found Niles and Elders cutting hardwood trim for the nearly finished lobby. The three men located a quiet corner and sat down on unopened five-gallon buckets of drywall mud.

"To me," Niles said, "the real question here is what kind of pictures do we want on the evening news? Right now, the pictures are going to be of this protest. If you go back, assuming anyone in the group would even recognize you, the pictures will include an angry mob huddled around you, reporters asking questions, and your white face saying something stupid like, 'no comment.' I think you are better off if you stay here."

"Thanks for your confidence in me," laughed Person.

"Mitch, he may be right," added Elders. "Today, Walker is looking for TV coverage. He's been manipulating those cameras for years. He'll eat you alive if you get near him. Just give him what he wants...this time."

"What about our buildings?" asked Person.

"They'll be okay as long as none of our guys start anything," Elders continued. "Like I said, they're just looking to put their faces and their cause in people's living rooms tonight. As long as they aren't tearing things up, peoople will sympathize with them. Walker knows better than to let things get out of hand. I can't promise what will happen once Walker's team leaves, but our buildings should be safe for a while."

Niles jumped in. "Besides, TV reporters get bored quick. They wouldn't be around by the time you got back anyway. Hopefully, one or two of them will call to get your side of the story." He added nervously, "What are you going to tell them?"

"Hadn't really thought about it," Person answered.

"May I just suggest you keep in mind that sound bites on TV are about 10 or 15 seconds. You tend to talk longer than that."

"It's hard to explain our side of the story in 15 seconds."

"You don't have a choice, Mitch. Either you summarize it into a sound bite, or you rattle on about the truth and let them summarize it for you. I don't trust their translation of what you might say."

"Good point. I'll work on it." Person barely finished that statement before his portable phone rang.

The other two men patted him on the back and walked back to their tasks. As Person unfolded his phone to answer it, he reflected on the fact that he would be facing these reporters alone. No one would be answering them for him. His friends had offered "good luck," or some other form of support, but once it was established that it was ultimately Mitchell Person's problem, not one of them tried to solve it for him. As Person sought advice, they gave what they could, but then left him to sort through it all and make his own decision.

They made it clear that he would have to face this crisis alone. That's why he loved and respected his friends so much. He smiled with genuine gratitude as he turned on the phone.

SIXTEEN

On the screen, the anchorwoman was leading off the news. She was pretty enough to get attention, but not so pretty as to lose credibility.

"In the heart of downtown today, a civil rights group protested a local construction company for discriminatory payment policies," she began. "Channel 7's Ray Shanley has more."

The picture cut to the protesters walking in front of Person's Fine Woodworking. Shanley's voice-over cut in, "Washington City's Act Now organization charges that this construction company pays its African-American workers less that they would be paid if they were white."

Another angle of the same scene. "Act Now leader Rev. Benjamin Walker says Person's Fine Woodworking takes advantage of the African-Americans who live nearby and cannot afford transportation to higher-paying jobs. He says that because the workers are unable to leave, owner Mitchell Person is able to treat them like slaves and pay them less than they are worth."

Cut to Walker at the podium. "Our laws say you can't

hold a man as a slave. Our laws say you can't pay a man less money for his work just because of the color of his skin. Our laws say you can't discriminate. We follow the laws and we are waiting for the laws to be followed for us. How long must we wait?!"

Cut to close-up of Walker, apparently being interviewed by Shanley. Crowd is visible in the background. "This man has admitted in the paper that he is here for his own greed, profit and selfishness. That's intolerable."

Close up of Person's sign. Shanley's voice over added, "When reached by phone, Person's response was simply that greed is bad but profit is good so he is not ashamed to be seeking profits."

Cut to Shanley in front of Person's Fine Woodworking, crowd visible in the back. "Walker says no lawsuit has been filed yet because no specific law has been broken. State Representative Seth Howard says the situation may not be illegal, but it is still wrong, especially because Person's company receives enterprise zone tax breaks. He says he is planning to introduce legislation requiring enterprise zone businesses to pay a reasonable wage.

"In Laughton Park, this is Ray Shanley, Channel 7 news."

Sandy Davis shook her head and ignored the rest of the news. Watching her dad operate all those years, she understood how the media game worked. As with most stories on the news, there were probably a dozen people in the city who really knew what was going on. The battle was always to see which of those people could best distort the news in their favor.

Television was usually the easier medium to manipulate.

There were fewer reporters than at a newspaper, which meant less of a chance that a TV reporter would have enough expertise in your issue to ask really tough questions. There was a bigger reliance on pictures. And stations were in hotter competition for rating points. Therefore, whichever side could make their story easily understood by the reporters, and with catchier phrases and pictures, would win that round of the media war.

She knew Mitch was probably not interested in competing in, let alone winning, the media game, so he was going to be dead meat if this issue kept going. Ever since she read the morning paper she had worried about him. She didn't call him, though. She figured his work would be better therapy than her call of support. But she desperately wanted to talk to him now.

The phone rang and she jumped up to get it, somewhat relieved. "Hello?"

"Hi honey. How are you doing?" said the phone back to her. Right words, wrong voice.

"Oh, hi Dad. Not too bad." Not sure why he called, she added, "Is everything okay with mom and the boys?"

"Yes, yes they're fine. I just wanted to call, uh, to, uh, see if you're doing all right. You know, I, uh, read about one of your friends in the paper today. I, uh, wondered if your feelings are hurt or something." Davis was having a hell of a time.

In a way, Sandy got a kick out of the fact that her all-powerful father was nervous around her. On the other hand, she felt badly that they didn't share a normal father-daughter relationship, if such a thing existed. She did her best not to take advantage of her power over him, partly because she didn't understand it, and partly because he *was* her father after all.

However, this phone call was suspicious. She was tempted to weasel some information about his involvement in the evolving fiasco at Laughton Park. She decided not to toy with her dad, though she was also determined not to reveal any information to him either.

"Thanks for the thought Dad, but I'm alright. Mr. Person is a solid man. He can handle it," She thought a moment, wanting to get it off her chest without saying anything revealing, then added, "It's a shame the way it's escalating. It was on the news tonight, you know."

"No, I didn't see it," he lied.

"Yeah, well, you know how those things go."

The line was silent for a moment as the two thought about what they were feeling versus what they should say.

Ron Davis spoke first. "There's a bright, young man working his way up through my company. I've had my eye on him and I keep thinking of you. If you wanted, I could..."

"No thanks Dad," she laughed. "I haven't had much luck with your picks of men. I appreciate the thought though."

"I keep trying," he laughed. "I might find the right one yet."

She almost blurted out, "and you might be too late," but didn't.

After another awkward pause, he added, "This thing won't

hurt your job will it? I mean, I know how proud you are of your relationship with your clients. This won't cause them to...I don't know...lose their trust, I guess?"

He was sincere this time, it was obvious to her, and it touched her. She knew he really wanted her to be happy in her work. He tried so hard to help her out, and it bothered him that she was only happy doing something of which he had no part. Despite his disappointment over her refusal to work with him or anything he touched, he was proud of her dedication to her work. She sensed now that he was worried he had botched her career.

Sure, with that last comment, he revealed to her that he knew what Seth Howard and Ben Walker were doing in Laughton Park, but he also revealed that he cared about how it affected her. The man made his career out of stomping on others. She had always known that when a person must hurt others to get ahead, sooner or later, they must hurt someone they love. She felt pity for her father, because he just realized he was on the verge of hurting his own daughter, and it bothered him deeply.

"Dad, I'll be fine. Thanks for your concern." It hadn't occurred to her yet that there might be some fallout with her clients because of her relationship with Mitch. But she wasn't too worried. Like Mitch, she didn't base her happiness on the opinions of others. She was proud of the clients that she was able to reach, the ones who discovered their own self-importance. But they would not rule her life. Only she could do that.

"Well, uh, let me know if you need to talk or anything." What a ludicrous statement. Like she was suddenly going to open up to him because he was screwing over her boyfriend. Mentally, he kicked himself.

"You too, Dad," she said, letting him know any other information would be appreciated.

They talked about upcoming holiday plans, about how her mother was doing, about what her brothers were up to. The conversation ended amicably.

The instant she hung up the phone, it rang again. She picked it up.

"Sandy? Mitch. How was your day today?"

She was relieved, though not surprised, to hear him in good spirits. "My day was fine. And yours?"

"Oh, pretty dull. Not much happened," he laughed.

"That's nice. I understand you had a few visitors at your shop today."

"Yes. A few gentlemen stopped by to express their excitement over my business success."

They let this die. Then she said, "Mitch, I'm glad you called. How are you doing, really."

"Not bad, believe it or not. It's nice to talk to a friendly voice though. I've been on the phone with reporters all afternoon. It was tough to get much accomplished. I tried to call you a couple of times this evening, but the line was busy."

"My dad called. He wanted to make sure I'm okay in spite of this negative publicity about you."

"That's nice of him. I hope you gave him my love."

"Funny. Listen, his call was a little weird. I've never told him or anyone connected with him about you and me. So how the hell did he know?"

"Father's intuition?"

"Father's investigation, more likely. I think they've had their eye on you for a while. He keeps a private investigator on retainer and I think they've been gathering information to use for plotting against you."

"What a waste of time. He could have just walked into my office and asked me what he wanted to know. I would have told him. My business is up-front and honest."

"There were a few people hanging around your front door today who might take exception with that."

"That's true." Person thought for a moment. "I'm in a bit of a bind."

Now there's an understatement, thought Sandy. "So it would seem. How do you see it?"

"I'm driven by a dedication to myself. I must create things that give me pride, that satisfy my ego. It's a pretty simple philosophy and it seems to be the same one that should guide everyone. But Travis keeps telling me that it's not a popular philosophy. The more I defend myself with what I am, the more enemies I make."

"Travis knows what he's talking about," Sandy said. "Are you going to change your tune?"

"Of course not. The bottom line is that I don't care what

your dad thinks about me. I don't care about the opinions of the media, Rev. Walker or anybody else. I appreciate the approval of you and Harry Tom, Travis and the other people who respect my work, but I don't expect or demand your approval.

"I like being around you, but when I look in the mirror, I don't see your face looking at me," he continued. "No matter how much time I spend with other people, ultimately, I'm alone with my own soul. I can't hide behind you or anyone else to escape my own soul. It's always with me."

"Sure. But why sacrifice your company when you could save it by playing their game? You could still be true to yourself, but just say the things they want to hear, whether you or any of your workers believe it or not."

"We talked about that in the break room today. If we worked on it, I'm sure we could put together a public relations campaign to save our investments. We voted against it though, unanimously. It's baffling to me that people would rather us put on a front for them. They want us to tell them what they want to hear rather than what is true. In the end we decided that to cave in to their needs would require us to change our actions for their benefit. We won't do that."

"This negative publicity is going to make it tough for you to find clients for any of your businesses. Are you really willing to let Laughton Park go out of business and fall into the same sad state of disrepair as before?" she asked.

"As nice and well-renovated as they are, the buildings in Laughton Park are only a shell keeping the rain off the men and women who are fulfilling their need for creation and accomplishment. Self-fulfillment is the real heart of Laughton Park.

"If I am driven out of my company by people who are uncomfortable with self-fulfillment, then so be it. I would rather go back to building yard barns on my own terms than own a large company that is afraid of offending the insecure.

"Once the selfish drive is taken out of Laughton Park, the buildings are already destroyed, regardless of how long it actually takes them to physically deteriorate."

After a moment of reflection, Sandy said, "It looks like I will be getting some of my old clients back. I can't say I'm happy about that."

"Really, it's up to them, Sandy. They have tasted the glory of their own egos. Who knows where they may go if Laughton Park dies again. On the other hand, Laughton Park might survive this."

"Do you think your companies might ride out this storm?"

"Why try to predict the future? Why give up because of what 'might' happen?" Then he added, "There is one thing I would like to happen in the near future. It involves me visiting your apartment tonight."

She smiled. "I'll predict that in the near future your wishes will come true." She pictured the two of them in their naked embrace. It was the one time when they truly released themselves to anyone. Those moments were cherished.

"Great. One last thing...are you content when you look in the mirror?"

She was shocked at the question. "Of course," she exclaimed. The only thing she was sure about in life was who she is.

"Even though you don't have great power over large numbers of people? Even though you don't turn the wheels of society? You're still content with yourself?"

Where was he going with these questions? "Look, Mitch. You're not the only one who can get by without the approval of others. I've turned down many opportunities to be 'a player' in the game. I'm perfectly happy with who I am. I can go to the mirror, look myself squarely in the eye, and smile because I see a woman who is not ashamed of her faith in herself."

"What does your dad see when he looks in the mirror?"

The line was silent for a while. He added, "I'll see you in a few minutes."

For the second time that night, Sandy felt pity for her father.

SEVENTEEN

When Person arrived at his office early the next morning, he saw Willie Bender scrubbing the outside wall. It wasn't unusual for Bender to be at the office before him. The young man was eager and dedicated. However, Person couldn't figure out what he was doing.

"Hey Willie, how are you doing."

"Not bad, Mitch. Just trying to get rid of some unwanted decoration."

As Person approached his colleague, he saw that the man was trying to scrub off a message painted by late-night vandals. The letters that were quickly fading under the elbow grease of Bender read, "KKK."

Person was stunned. When he first opened Person's fine woodworking, his building was a frequent target of gang logos and other graffiti. He kept cleaning off the messages or painting over them. As he continued the renovation of his building and expanding to the others, the graffiti began to taper off. Eventually, as the Laughton Park development became more successful, the graffiti stopped.

This was the first message in over a year. And it was a particularly nasty one. He grabbed a brush and joined Bender's efforts. In no time, the letters were gone. The two men walked into their building.

"Willie, how bad is it?" Person had tried to say something encouraging to each of his employees yesterday. He got to most of them, and they all seemed genuinely supportive. But he knew the more Walker screamed about civil rights, the more his workers would be put under confusing pressure.

"You don't got to worry about me, Mitch. I know what you're about. I think most of the brothers feel the same way. It's going to get tough though. You holding up?"

"Yeah. That paint-job bothers me. I don't really care what they call me or what they do to me, but I wish they wouldn't do things to make the other workers uncomfortable." He thought about that for a second. "On the other hand, this company is the people who work here. They can't very well do anything to the company without doing something to the people."

With that, he wandered to his office, deep in thought.

Today was payday at Person's Fine Woodworking. Several months ago, Rudy Jefferson sold Person on a system whereby Brothers' Printing would run off the bi-weekly payroll checks for his company. Jefferson had invested in a software program that he could combine with one of his new check forms to handle the process easily, quickly and more efficiently than Person was able to do in the past, and with the same level of confidentiality. Part of the contract was that Rudy would have the checks ready for Person early enough on payday that the workers could get their money before going out to the job site.

Person waited for the checks. His crew had been working long hours lately to try and finish the Benham United project. They were almost done. Despite the constant flow of workers to and from Benham, Person expected everyone to come to the shop this morning to get their check. He decided it was time to talk to them.

Word was spread among the workers that this week, they were to report to the break room for their pay. The room was just big enough to hold everyone, though some people had to do without chairs. They made do by sitting on available counter space or upside-down buckets.

When everyone was in the break room, Person came in with the money. He worked his way to the table in the middle of the room and climbed on top. The room grew quiet.

He held aloft the checks. "I've got your measly checks, you poor wretched, oppressed creatures." A chuckle swept through the group. It was not that funny of a joke, but they were relieved to see their boss in good spirits.

"Since yesterday, many of you have come to me to offer your support. I appreciate that." He was serious again. "But we all know this is ultimately my problem. However, I am beginning to realize that whatever happens to me will have some effect on you.

"I didn't plan it that way. But that's the way it's working out. The company has always been open. I share my plans with you and you share your suggestions with me. So I better tell you what I think about this company's future.

"As always, I'm committed to my own achievements and development. Everyone in this room understands that, because we all share the same belief. You were hired to join this operation because you have that inner fire that makes you to want to create physical testimonies to your pride, your soul. I believe you are dedicated to your own egos, that is why I trust you.

"Some companies don't have that same belief in their workers. They don't welcome their workers' input in business decisions. Some workers don't share your dedication to themselves and to quality. In those shops, no one trusts anyone else. They can't. Everyone tries to get ahead, but they try to succeed by pulling others behind them, not by striving to be better," The men in the room who had worked in other shops nodded their agreement.

Person continued, "What's the difference between those shops and ours? The difference is that in this shop, we are not ashamed to say we want to be better than everyone else. We are not ashamed to say we want to make a profit. We are not ashamed to say we do our work for our own benefit.

"It's human nature to work for one's own benefit. That's how man has survived all these years. It's the undeniable force of life. Why then are those other shops afraid to admit that they are doing things for themselves? Probably because they have looked at their work and cannot be proud of it." A few in the room chuckled.

"Our self-dedication is threatening to those who cannot be proud of their own creations. The more our projects invade their lives, the more they are forced to face what they have done. Some of the people we have made uncomfortable have the power to rally their forces against us.

"Right now, we are fine. But *they* are the creators of the laws that govern us, so eventually, they may be able to affect us. That leaves us with two choices. First, I can find out what they want and give in to it. I can say what they want me to say, or bring in the union or hire anyone who wants a job rather than anyone we want to hire. The second choice is to remain true to our principles and be willing to let them kill the company rather than kill ourselves by giving in.

"Personally, I will hand them the key to this building before I will hammer one nail to help them further their cause. I must be true to myself. I know no other way. Let them drive me out of business. I really don't care. I can always go back to building yard barns on my own terms. I enjoy this company, but it is not my life. *I* am my life. My spirit goes with me, but this building cannot move. Therefore, my dedication is to my spirit. As long as each of us can bring our spirits to this building, the company should stay. But if this becomes a place where spirits are broken, then it is nothing more than a shelter from the wind and rain.

"I hope this works out in our favor. I hope that explains to you where we stand today."

The room was quiet as each man and woman

contemplated his or her own future. What would have surprised most people is that no one in the room was resentful that they might soon lose their jobs. Most of them had been unemployed before. And all of them shared Person's will to work on their own terms rather than for the benefit of a fellow union worker. This proud selfishness was the common thread that ran through the room.

Person began again. "In the earliest civilizations, the weather could make a man cold. Some men decided they could stay warm by stealing furs from other men. Some men decided there must be a better way and eventually discovered fire."

Looking around the break room, he added, "Let's leave the blanket and go finish stoking the fire over at Benham United."

With that, the crew cheered and rose to collect their checks before heading out the door. As an orator, Person was not in the same league as Rev. Walker or Seth Howard, but he got the point across. And his workers really appreciated his message.

Willie Bender stayed at the back of the line. He looked a little nervous as he approached Person.

"Mitch, Rev. Walker ain't that bad of a guy. He just feels he gots to jump on any cause that come along."

"Maybe so, Willie, but it bothers me that a person would take on any cause, whether good or bad, just to stay visible," Person replied.

"You're right, but it may be good to talk to him. My cousin has his ear. I think he could set up a meeting if you want."

Harry Tom overheard the conversation and joined in.

"That may not be a bad idea, Mitch. We shouldn't throw in the towel until we at least talk to the guy." Then he laughed and added. "We know for a fact that Ron Davis is an asshole and Seth Howard is an asshole. Might as well find out for a fact if Ben Walker is an asshole too."

The three men laughed. Person asked Willie if he would set it up.

****

Behind a dry-cleaning shop in the trendy part of town, way across the city from Laughton Park, sat the offices of the Washington City *Endurance*. With the motto "The truth will endure, sooner or later, if you're patient, and if you look for it," the *Endurance* was the city's alternative newspaper.

The paper's philosophy, and that of the few reporters who could afford to work there for a meager salary, was that the real story was rarely revealed in the regular media. Generally, they felt, the more cynical one was about reports in the mainstream paper, the closer one would be to knowing what was really going on.

Like other alternative newspapers in the country, the *Endurance* operated on a shoestring budget. Their pages of satire and cynicism, though based on accurate reporting, attracted a small but elite following. Therefore, they had trouble getting large advertisers to support their efforts. They could, however, depend on enough support from smaller, more targeted companies to keep every issue coming out.

*Un*like most other alternative newspapers in the country, the *Endurance* did not automatically embrace liberal issues. Instead, they were more libertarian in their leanings, attacking attempted government intrusions whether by Republicans, Democrats or Independents.

Nearly every politician and agency head in state and local government had been attacked at one time or another in the pages of the paper. Because of its ruthlessness, the paper was hated by every government and political leader, though it was read, each week, cover to cover, by all of them. Although the readership was small, it was influential. Yet, due to the *Endurance's* tendency to berate its most powerful readers, the paper had no influence on these people. The second-tier workers in government loved the paper, though, because it reflected government operations the way they saw them. They were loyal readers.

One thing the *Endurance* reporters detested was attempted "spin" by the subjects of their stories. They felt that the reason mainstream papers were inaccurate was because many mainstream reporters depended on stories that were fed to them by press secretaries. Sure, those reporters usually checked facts with independent sources and tried to find opposing quotes, but the resulting story was still primarily the creation of someone's press office.

A few times, a politician or his press secretary would make the mistake of calling the *Endurance* to plant a story or try to "correct" something that was printed in an earlier issue. Rather than politely declining the "help," the *Endurance* would tape record the conversation and print it verbatim in its paper.

One time, they discovered that they were subjected to the same spin as the *Times-Union*. The difference was that the spin worked on the mainstream paper. Gleefully, the *Endurance* printed excerpts from the *Times-Union* story side-by-side with the spin phone call they had received, illustrating how the "spin doctor" affected the news as reported by the *Times-Union*.

Sam Janus was proud of his paper. He sat calmly in his office, finally desensitized to the smell of dry-cleaning chemicals that permeated the wall from the storefront shop, and read through other papers. This week's *Endurance* was on the press, and he used the time to catch up on what other papers in the city and across the state were doing. Sometimes, these papers gave him ideas of stories that needed some digging.

His office was not very fancy. In fact it was cluttered and eclectically decorated, like most news offices in the country. The building itself was dark and drab, but it was in the trendy part of town. Janus felt it gave his paper credibility to be headquartered where the supposedly brighter people lived, despite the fact that they were his main targets. The dingy office was the only one in this part of town that he could afford, so he and his reporters put up with the alley view and the smell of dry-cleaning.

Suddenly, as he flipped through a two-day-old issue of the *Times-Union*, he froze. A photograph of two well-dressed white guys talking to some ratty-looking African-American caught his attention, as it had many of the residents of Washington City. Janus quickly read the caption and the accompanying story. To him this photo was more significant than it had been for most people.

He grabbed his phone book and flipped through the pages with one hand as he reached for his phone with the other. It was 10:30 p.m., a little late to call most people, but Janus didn't care. He got some of his best information when he called people at home, late in the evening.

When the phone was answered, Janus said, "I always knew attorneys would do just about anything for publicity, but reviving slavery is going a bit too far."

The line was silent. Janus smiled as he pictured the wheels turning in the head of the other man.

Finally, Travis Niles said, "Sam?" The laugh on the other end of the line was the only confirmation Niles needed. "Sam Janus, how the hell are you?" he exclaimed.

"Pretty good, Travis. Just working away. Funny thing is, I don't pay my people very well either but I can't get my picture in the *Times-Union*."

"Jeeze, what a mess this thing has become. As you can guess, the *Times-Union* doesn't have it exactly right. No surprise. Hey, how's that rag of yours doing. I read it every week."

"Thanks for your weekly half-dollar. It helps buy the coffee."

Niles and Janus were roommates in college. Janus in journalism and Niles in political science, as pre-law. The two hit it off perfectly, because they shared the same inquiring spirit and faith in the human soul. Janus, however, was much more cynical in his approach. He warned Niles that the young political science major would not like the legal profession. Years later, when Niles found himself spending more time working with wood than chasing billable hours, he reflected on Janus' comments. The two had kept in close contact shortly after graduation but had slowly drifted apart with time.

"I laughed my ass off when I saw you were the editor of the *Endurance*," Niles said. "We all read that thing religiously at the law firm. I told people that I roomed with you. They were kind of suspicious of me anyway. Man, I wanted to call and see how you were doing."

"Why didn't you?"

Niles laughed. "I didn't want to see my phone call in your damn paper."

"Yeah, our phone doesn't ring very often these days. It makes it tough to find leads, but it also cuts out all the crap."

The reunited friends started chit-chatting, reminiscing over college stories and expressing no surprise that neither had found the right woman yet.

Finally, Janus said, "It's good to talk to you again, Travis, but my call wasn't only for pleasure."

"So I figured."

"Can we get together for a beer? I'd like to talk to you about this Laughton Park stuff."

"It would be nice to have an open mind take a look at this thing. It's getting messy and it's only going to get worse." Niles knew Janus wouldn't jump on the bandwagon to crucify Person, though he wouldn't hesitate to add to the abuse if he thought it was justified. Niles figured it was worth the risk to bring his old friend into the fold. Besides, he wanted to see his college roommate again.

"I was suspicious as soon as I saw the byline on the story. Aaron Teldon is a real piece of shit," said Janus. Then he laughed, "That doesn't mean you aren't one too, but it makes me curious about what's really going on."

They made plans to meet after work the next day.

****

The media was having fun. The legislature wasn't due to reconvene for a few more weeks. There hadn't been a good fire or bank robbery for awhile. Not much was happening...except the potential riot in Laughton Park.

No one in the media would go so far as to provoke anything, but they were watching with keen interest. The media hated racists, and rightfully so, so they were usually ready to jump behind Rev. Walker and point the public spotlight where he directed it. Once, before Walker had gained much savvy, he made the mistake of pointing out the lack of African-American news anchors and reporters in the Washington City media. His accusations got only minor coverage and a few editorials accused him of stirring trouble just to generate publicity. He learned quickly that it was stupid to punch holes in your own boat.

To get in on the Laughton Park action, Ron Davis had started his letters-to-the-editor machine. The ACC never had any trouble with the *Times-Union*, but some of the other media outlets occasionally criticized the union's tactics, especially during strikes. If a newspaper published a negative story about union workers, Davis' public relations manager would write several response letters. He kept a list of people who were willing to sign and mail any ACC letter to any paper. The PR manager would simply contact the person whose turn it was, send the letter to the person via courier, and that person would sign it and drop it in the mail that day.

A few years ago, one of the more conservative newspapers in the state lambasted the ACC for demanding an 11 percent salary increase during a recession when many companies were forced to either cut salaries or lay off workers. For the next two weeks, that paper's editorial page was filled with responses, slamming the paper for being unsympathetic to workers' rights, talking about the extreme wealth of business owners, and threatening to boycott advertisers. The paper never recanted its statement, but it never criticized the ACC again.

At that same time, Davis Construction Company was in fierce competition with another large construction firm. Davis immediately granted the 11 percent salary boost to his workers, which made the ACC employees at the other shop even more adamant for their raise. The other firm negotiated and eventually settled on a 9 percent hike. Shortly afterward, the economy took another downturn, slowing the construction industry. Davis' competitor could not make the payroll and was forced out of business. Davis picked up most of their pending contracts, making Davis Construction the undisputed construction giant in the state.

Knowing that Davis and the ACC were virtually one in the same, some people quietly questioned whether the entire strike and salary demand were orchestrated by Davis as a quest for power. People wondered how Davis maintained a cash flow during the economic downturn that affected his business as much as that of his competitor. Also, people wondered why the ACC accepted only 3 percent salary increases from Davis each of the next two years. Of course no one, except the *Endurance*, ever questioned this out loud, but it didn't have much influence.

For the Laughton Park situation, letters began to trickle into the *Times-Union* and other papers. Some letters sharply criticized Person for taking advantage of his employees. Other letters claimed that Laughton Park was an example of why the country needed a strong labor union.

The letters were not an attempt to create a story, because the issue was receiving adequate coverage. Rather, they were just an attempt to make sure the union message was not lost in the debate.

While Aaron Teldon was following the directions of Rev. Walker and Seth Howard, some of the other reporters were looking for their own angles. One TV reporter found a few people who applied for jobs in Laughton Park, but were turned down. Those rejects had plenty to say about how unfair Person was. Many reporters tried to talk to Person's employees, but his workers chose not to comment.

One reporter went into Brothers' Printing to talk to Rudy Jefferson about his now-famous neighbor. Jefferson duly pointed out to the reporter that if it wasn't for Person, he wouldn't own this print shop and most of the people working in Laughton Park would be drawing unemployment.

"Look at those men going in and out of the construction shop. Look at them over at the paint shop. Can't you see it in their eyes? They love their jobs. They love what they're doing," Jefferson told the reporter. "They don't care they ain't getting union wages. Many of them left that damn union 'cause they wasn't treated right. But now they got a chance to do what they want to do, the way they want to do it, and they're proud."

When the reporter ran those comments by one of Walker's men, the anti-Person activist pointed out to him that first of all, Jefferson was paying his workers below union scale too, and secondly, he was now a business owner in Laughton Park, a co-conspirator, despite the color of his skin.

In all fairness, the reporter gave equal coverage to both sets of comments, but Jefferson didn't like the way his side of the story played out. He decided not to speak to reporters any more.

The day after the first protest outside Person's Fine Woodworking, Walker decided to stage another march just to keep the issue alive. Davis' PR manager convinced Davis to send some ACC representatives, white and Black, to join in the fray.

Over the years, the ACC had also suffered from accusations of racism. Years before Ron Davis' rise to power, the union bosses recognized the potential influx of new dues that would result from an increased workforce. The labor group helped push through civil rights legislation that would bring more African-Americans into the work place. However, people began to notice years later that although African-Americans were welcomed into the union shops, they were not advancing very fast.

Like most unions, the ACC followed a strong seniority system. Raises and promotions were granted on the basis of tenure. Because African-Americans were newer to the union, there were many White men who were due to get promotions before any Black would be eligible. Furthermore, during layoffs, the last-hired, first-fired provisions of most union contracts tended to harm African-Americans disproportionately.

Rev. Walker and Act Now worked with the union to try and correct the problem. But the union was slow to act, though it did its best to demonstrate progress to Walker. Eventually, the ACC finalized some plans to throw out the seniority system and replace it with a "worker quality" system, which would be granted by supervisors.

Ironically, this change was scheduled to take place at about the time that African-American union members were finally in line to receive seniority promotions. Furthermore, the supervisors who would be making the decisions about the new "worker quality" system were all white. Walker didn't buy it for a minute and threatened the ACC with public denouncements. The union backed off its plans to try and appease him. Negotiations were still ongoing between the ACC and Walker.

Davis' sharp PR manager recognized the Laughton Park

affair as a chance to heal some wounds with African-Americans. After all, this situation was a perfect combination of perceived anti-Black and anti-union problems. At the PR man's urging, the union decided to join hands with Walker in an attempt to be seen as the protector of civil rights as well as worker rights.

The latest protest worked beautifully for the ACC. White men, wearing ACC caps and jackets, were holding anti-racist signs, marching next to Black activists. It made for good TV.

That evening, the Benham United project was finished. As usual, the work was excellent. To the trained eye, the care and workmanship was obvious. It screamed out from the walls, the floors, the woodwork, the paint job. A craftsman could walk through the renovation and feel like he was in a temple to his trade.

To the untrained eye, the quality was less obvious. It was more a feeling of comfort. One felt secure walking about the offices, like the building was a solid security blanket.

This project should have been the one to propel Person's Fine Woodworking and the other Laughton Park businesses into the big time. Most of their projects were a much smaller scale, awarded because the client happened to notice and appreciate one of Person's other projects. The number of these smaller projects was growing, but Person wanted some larger projects to serve as a testimony to quality that would touch more people.

The Benham renovation proved that Person could perform the same intimate quality associated with his home and small office renovations on a large scale. He was negotiating with a couple of other bigger companies currently. The completed Benham project should have been his trump card.

Unfortunately, other companies' decisions were not based solely on quality. The day after the first protest, one of the companies Person was negotiating with called to say they were no longer interested in his bid. He knew the other would also be reconsidering whether it wanted to take a risk with the controversy confronting his shop.

Person's problem was that he hired additional workers for the Benham project with hope that he could attract other big projects to keep them busy. Unless he could either solve the controversy quickly or find large companies that were not affraid of the protests, he would have to begin laying off workers for the first time in the short life of his business.

To him, the sadness of this prospect did not stem from his consideration of the effect of layoffs on his workers. Rather, it was the disappointment that fewer projects would be undertaken with quality and personal accomplishment as their goal.

EIGHTEEN

Because he was working late to complete the Benham United project, Niles was late for his meeting with Sam Janus. The editor of the *Endurance* didn't mind though. He used the time to watch people, peruse a couple newspapers he brought along, write some notes, and drink a cold draft.

When Niles finally came in, Janus laughed at him. The former attorney's hair was still wet from taking a quick shower and hurrying over. His clothes were rumpled as if they had been grabbed off the floor and thrown on, which is exactly what had happened.

Janus signaled the waiter to bring a beer for his friend and got up to extend a hand to his old friend. The two men shook hands, then hugged. Truly glad to see each other again after so many years, they settled into their seats to enjoy each other's company and get caught up on the last few years.

The reporter explained how he had left the mainstream press after only a year. He worked at the largest paper in a different city. Graduated with a minor in economics, Janus had been assigned to a business beat for the paper. He enjoyed some success and praise for his insight into the complexities of the issues. But he was not happy.

"The lifeblood of a newspaper or radio station or TV news team is the news tip. Eventually, all the media end up reporting the same thing, but the reporter that gets the tip, and the story, first is the winner," he explained to Niles. "We are always looking for a hot tip or a new angle that draws customers to our paper or station instead of the other guy's.

"In the end, it's just a business. We want to attract the largest, most loyal readership or viewership so we can sell more advertising. The marketing departments handle a good part of that, but to the journalists, we need tips to do our part for the success of our paper or station.

"The thing is, most other industries know that about the media. The businesses I covered sent me tips all the time, trying to get me to cover some positive aspect of their business. They wanted free publicity from me. Positive coverage in a newspaper is much more important than an advertisement in a newspaper because a news story has credibility that no ad can match. If some reader looks at an advertisement, he knows the company paid to put it in there. He knows the company had complete control of the words and pictures in the ad. He knows the company put the ad in the paper to try to influence him. So he treats the ad cautiously.

"But if he reads a positive story about the company, he assumes the reporter's praise for the company is based on fact. He thinks the reporter stumbled upon the company because it was so good it stood out from the rest. He'll read the story and get a much more in-depth look at the company than he would from a brief ad. If the story turns out the way the company hoped, he feels good about the company and its product.

"Of course, reporters also cover the negative aspect of companies. We reveal the big polluters, the tax evaders and the other unsavory characters. The reader reads one of those stories and he gets a deep negative feeling about a company.

"What do you suppose happens if a company that sells toothpaste wins a positive story for itself and a negative story for the other companies that sell toothpaste? They've helped themselves and it didn't cost them one dime of advertising money.

"Businesses have a big stake in what is printed in the business section. In fact, they probably read it more than the general public they are trying to influence. But in any case, they each try to have the best public relations staff to keep the positive stories coming about themselves and the negative stories about their competitors.

"After a few months at the paper, I realized that the volume of tips that we were getting from businesses made it tough to dig up anything on our own from other sources. We spent all our time evaluating the tips we got and following up on the promising ones. We couldn't ignore any of the tips, because our competitor might find a big story there and beat us to it.

"That started to bother me. I mean, I viewed journalism as the unbiased outside source of news. And I think most reporters do their best to keep the stories as objective as possible. But Travis, how objective can you be in a story when the story itself was generated by a company that wanted that story in your paper?

"I began looking around at the other departments. The government beat. The police beat. Features. The entertainment beat, they were the worst. All these reporters in all these departments were having their agendas dictated to them by the industries they covered.

"Then it hit me, this is what reporting is all about. The news media is a reactive entity. If a business or a politician creates news, it is the reporter's duty to cover it. There are news makers in every community. Whatever they do is deemed newsworthy, so reporters have to follow their lead. Maybe in the old days the media could influence the agenda, but that is back when papers were more biased and played a bigger advocacy role.

"Now the public and policy makers demand the media to be less biased. The media merely reacts rather than acts. They have relinquished agenda-setting to industry and government. Ironically, news reporting can't be truly objective when the news is purposely and subjectively created by someone else. The price of increased objectivity has been reduced objectivity.

"I guess there's nothing wrong with that. Fortunately, the agenda-setters frequently oppose each other, and that tends to even out the coverage. But it is not the picture I got of the media from journalism school. It's not what I was interested in.

"A couple of times, I took a lead farther than the company wanted. I found out exactly why they were pushing some angle of a story. It was usually to cover their own ass. So I reported what

I found. At first my editors praised me for my hard work. The companies, of course, hated my guts, but that was okay because I had the backing of my paper. But an interesting thing happened. The tips started trickling off. Companies were afraid of what I might do to them, so they stopped giving me information. I thought that was great. I finally had a chance to take charge of my agenda. I could get business leads from outside the business section. Journalism was fun again.

"Unfortunately, the tips from the companies kept flowing to our competitors. They were printing stories that we didn't have. This made my editors unhappy. I tried to explain that it was due to my in-depth coverage and my unwillingness to kiss a business' ass. They either didn't understand the connection, or didn't care. Sensing I was losing their support, I knew I would have to go back to the old way of reporting if I wanted a future at that paper.

"I decided I had to be true to myself. I quit and moved to Washington City to start the *Endurance*."

Janus realized he had been talking a while, probably revealed more about himself to his friend than he had to anyone else. Averting his eyes to the floor, he sat back and re-moisturized his throat with a long drink of beer.

Niles took it all in with keen interest. He had read the *Endurance* for years and always wondered why his roommate created it. Like most other people in the city, Niles relied on the daily paper for news about the city and for information relevant to his field. When he worked for the law firm, he knew he had to read at least one daily paper every day and watch the evening news or else he risked missing out on information that other attorneys had. There was as much competition within his firm as there was with other firms.

The *Endurance* was a different case. Not every attorney in the city read it, or at least admitted to reading it. Some feigned a sense of pride that would prevent them from reading "that rag." But Niles quickly found the information in his old friend's newspaper just as valuable as what he found in the dailies.

As a small-budget weekly paper, the *Endurance* didn't cover anywhere near the volume of news as other papers. Instead, it chose stories seemingly at random. What it provided was a look at the news behind the news. Working in a law firm in the state's capital, Niles knew that most stories were not what they seemed on the surface. He and his colleagues were always gossiping about what was "really" happening behind the scenes that lead to stories in the mainstream media. With the *Endurance*, they didn't have to guess. Janus' paper usually had the real story, only it might be a month or two after the story finally left the pages of a daily.

Some reporters dismissed the *Endurance* articles as mere speculation. But Niles trusted the reporting completely. He only wished the paper covered more stories and more quickly. But he knew the real stories took a long time to flush out, especially with a small staff and budget.

"I never miss and issue, Sam. I think you provide an important service to this city," Niles said. "I rely on the mainstream media, but over the years I have come to rely on your paper just as much." He chuckled, then added, "I hope business is good. I don't know where I'd get my juicy information if you close shop."

"It's going well enough," Janus replied. He looked back at his friend and smiled. He could tell his old friend still understood him. "Really, I consider myself very lucky. You said my paper performs a service for the city, but that's not why I started it. I did for myself. I'm just glad enough people buy the paper to allow me to keep it going."

"I know exactly how you feel," Niles said.

It was the former attorney's turn to tell his story to Janus. He explained how he had excelled in law school and been hired by one of the most powerful law firms in Washington City. Niles was on the fast track to a partner position, but he was beginning to feel uneasy with his career.

"Sam, it seemed the more I advanced, the less I actually did. And when I looked at the senior attorneys in our firm, they did even less than me.

"Here we were, a huge influential law firm. But did we really practice law? Most of our firm's operation had little to do with law and order. We did contracts, negotiations, lobbying, all that stuff. Most of our work was work that has been created over the years by attorneys for attorneys.

"I mean, why should some company have to hire a law firm to help them write a disclaimer or otherwise protect them against liability? It's because there is always some other firm in town that makes liability a real threat.

"So much of the field of law goes way beyond prosecuting a person who commits a crime against another citizen or defending a citizen who has been wrongly accused. That's the kind of law that the typical man on the street cares about. But that's not what we were doing in our firm.

"No, our clients were faceless corporations or state agencies who needed legal advice or contracts or God knows what. Sure there were crimes that were committed, but a lot of these crimes were what I call 'paper crimes.' Crimes that were created in the halls of the legislature to help some companies get an advantage over other ones. These laws that are created are so obscure that the general public can't understand them or give a shit about them. So why the hell do they exist?

"As an attorney, I shouldn't have cared. It meant big business for us. Some attorneys would be hired to draft some law to create one of these paper crimes. Then other attorneys would be hired to get it passed through the legislature. And still more attorneys would be hired by the target firms to help them figure out how to get around these laws. And not one of these new laws meant much of anything to companies in terms of the quality of product they produced.

"Now, I'm not knocking my old profession. It never bothered me that there were so many attorneys working at this pointless game. The field of law, like the media, is reactive. Attorneys are meeting a need in society, though it is sometimes a dark and destructive need.

"Like you, I had a revelation one day about what I was

doing. It occurred to me that the other attorneys and I were merely helping some companies gain an advantage over their competitors, not by out-producing them or making a better product, but by gaining some technical legal advantage.

"Whatever happened to the days when businesses competed with one another on the basis of what they made? I always thought businesses tried to find a product that people needed and then make it better than the other companies that made that product.

"Instead, I found out that the top business is not necessarily the best. It may just be the business with the best lawyers or PR staff. The struggle for superiority has moved beyond the marketplace and is now being fought in the halls of the statehouse and the courthouse. The lazy business making an inferior product has an equal chance of winning this battle.

"When I realized I was part of this process it made me sick. I had to get out of there. I thought about going into criminal law, you know, working for the prosecutor or something. But I talked to my friends who took that route and they told me all about plea bargains, unmanageable caseloads, political ambition and other things that didn't fit my naive image of law and order.

"I was sitting around the house, trying to figure out what to do when I noticed the bookshelves I had made several years ago. I had forgotten how much I loved working with wood. Creating things that would last long after I was gone. The smell of sawdust as a board is moved across a table saw. The feel of a board that you've just sanded as smooth as a baby's ass.

"Well, my student loans were paid, so I thought, 'Why not?' I would quit law as soon as I found a woodworking shop that I wanted to work in. One night I was in Miller's Tavern over on West 32nd Street, having a brew with some friends from the firm. It was my first time in that bar, and the minute I walked in, I was hit with the wondrous woodworking inside.

"You know how you can go in some bars and restaurants and the decor is kind of a forced ambiance? The fake pressed tin ceiling that's really made of plastic? The new wood trim that's supposed to look like the restaurant has been standing for a century, even though it's part of a strip mall that was build two years ago? Well, Miller's Tavern is nothing like that.

"The wood trim, the bar, the floor, the walls, they all worked together to say, 'This is Miller's Tavern. It looks like Miller's Tavern and only Miller's Tavern. It doesn't remind you of anything else, nor can anything else remind you of this.' I doubt if any of my friends noticed it, but I sure did. I asked the manager who build the place and he told me it was Person's Fine Woodworking and gave me a card.

"I resigned the next day and I've been with Mitch ever since."

Janus said, "It doesn't surprise me you are into woodworking. I remember those lofts you made for our dorm room. I bet they're still standing. And by the way, I've been in Miller's Tavern and I know what you're talking about. I love that place."

The two men sat for a few minutes, staring at their mugs

and at the half-eaten bowl of stale popcorn on their table. They reflected on how each had gone through similar experiences to bring them to where they were today.

After a bit, Janus looked at Niles and said, "He's getting screwed, isn't he?"

Niles shrugged. "The oddest thing is, he doesn't care. He could make a run at trying to save our companies, but he doesn't want to waste our time playing with Seth Howard or Ben Walker. He is too devoted to his craft. That's what makes him happy. The more we have discussed this thing, the more we have decided that it doesn't mean anything if they close Laughton Park. The real business is us, each individual, and unless they kill us, we can continue to work. It doesn't matter if we are together, or apart, or in Washington City, or in the Amazon region. Somewhere, somehow, we will find an opportunity to work for our own selfish need to create."

"I'm in kind of an awkward position, Travis. I never ask permission to run a story on something. But it's been such a long time since I've seen you, I would hate to piss you off on our reunion. I want to look into this for my paper."

Niles laughed. "I would love for you to write a story on this. The rule of thumb of me and everyone else employed in Laughton Park is that each man should be able to pursue what he wants. Not a soul there would fret about you digging around. I think it's pretty clear you are not going to stir up more trouble. I feel even more comfortable about it knowing your devotion to quality."

"Thanks for the complement, Travis. It means something coming from you," Janus said. "I'll need some information."

The two men talked until well past midnight.

NINETEEN

Apparently, Mitchell Person and Rev. Walker had a different understanding of what their meeting was to be. Person assumed the two men would meet privately, giving Person a chance to explain what was going on. He thought this would be an opportunity for Walker to step out of the spotlight and reevaluate his position on Laughton Park.

However, when the time came for the meeting, Person looked out the front of his building and saw Walker marching toward the front door, flanked by a couple of his aids and about four reporters. "And to think I took time away from my tools for this," thought Person.

Walker had noticed that media attention was beginning to dwindle. He was running out of angles, and he knew Seth Howard was planning a news conference to introduce legislation tomorrow. At first, Walker planned on a cordial and private meeting with Person, but now he knew this was his last chance to grab media attention before he would have to relinquish the spotlight to Howard. Walker would continue to be involved in the issue, but he knew the focus of media coverage would shift to the legislative angle, where Howard would lead.

That morning he decided to call Aaron Teldon, a couple of TV guys and the reporter from the Black-oriented radio station to accompany him.

"Mr. Person, I'm Rev. Benjamin Walker here for our scheduled meeting," he was putting on quite a show of importance. "I hope you do not mind that I have asked members of the media to attend. I believe this is a vital issue affecting the African-Americans in this community. What we discuss here today may serve as a turning point in race relations in this city. Therefore, our words will be too important to hide behind closed doors."

Person was fascinated with the man's performance. He respected his ability to use words, but he wondered where the man's heart was. Not interested in attempting an equally stuffy demeanor, Person casually said, "No problem, I understand. And please call me Mitch."

That caught Walker off guard a bit, though he hid it from his aids and the reporters. Also, there was something about this man's eyes that he had not anticipated. He expected the man to act belligerent, to close the door in his face (which would make great TV coverage for Walker's cause), or to act guilty and uncomfortable. Instead, this Mitchell Person was completely at ease and confident. His eyes drove right through Walker, quickly evaluating his soul to see what kind of man he was.

Walker could tell that Person's evaluation was not in the civil rights leader's favor. The man who commanded the respect of thousands of city residents was instantly written off by a mere construction worker. What bothered Walker was that he could tell the evaluation had nothing to do with skin color. This construction worker looked at him to judge not what he is saying or doing, but what he *is*. But how could he fail a test based on values and beliefs?

Another irritation to Walker was the way Person handled his rejection of Walker. Instead of giving Walker a look of condescension, or reproach, or taking a defensive position, Person gave him a look of indifference. There was something about Walker he didn't like, but he didn't care enough to let it affect him.

Throughout his life, Walker faced many forms of racism. Some was the pure hatred by ignorant people who felt threatened by people of dark skin. These people were usually suffering from severe inferiority. They were secretly afraid that "even the niggers" were better than them. Walker usually had fun with these folks, because it was easy to keep them off guard, and most whites were as annoyed by these people as the African-Americans were. Any time these clowns staged a march or passed out racist literature, donations and calls of support flowed into Act Now headquarters.

Some racism he faced was the innocent racism by whites who just assumed they were superior and acted condescendingly toward African-Americans, though they didn't realize they were doing it. This was more common, and it was tougher to address because the people usually believed they were not racist. It was uncomfortable for these people to realize that they were in error, and that they should change.

Also, he faced a kind of institutional racism. Practices that had been in place for many years that tended to harm African-Americans more than whites. His toughest battles were in this arena, because it is difficult to change long-standing practices, especially when needed changes could sometimes result in reverse discrimination. Some affirmative action hiring reforms fell into this category. Walker knew some of the changes he had pushed ended up causing African-Americans to be hired simply because of their skin color. He was a little uneasy with the irony of using skin color to correct wrongs caused by years of people evaluating skin color, but he believed it was necessary to help society in the long run.

When he was confronted with Laughton Park, he figured it was the second kind of racism. He believed that Person was merely taking advantage of a situation where he could make money off African-American labor. He expected to see that kind of benevolent condescension on Person's face. The "I'm just trying to help you stupid brothers" look. But that piercing, probing glance was unlike anything he had experienced before.

He wanted to call it a new kind of racism. But he noticed Person looking at the white reporters the same way. He felt Person would have given the exact same evaluation of the white President of the United States if he had been standing here instead of Walker. The fact that Person was judging him based on his soul rather than the color of his skin made Walker feel odd. The fact that he apparently failed the test made him uncomfortable.

What if Person was indeed bringing new life to this neighborhood? Maybe he was onto something with his talk of self-reliance and profit motivation. If only he could talk to the man one-on-one and pick his brain a little bit, Walker thought. But it was too late for that. The stage was set. The reporters were there. And, after all, the ongoing struggle was more important than the career of one construction worker. Still, Walker had doubts about his role.

Fortunately, Walker trained himself to make the best of uncomfortable situations. He knew he would come out of here with a victory in the eyes of his aids and the media. But he knew it would be a hollow victory in his own mind.

The men gathered around a table in the break room, Person and Walker sitting next to each other, turned slightly so they would be facing. Deciding that dressing up certainly didn't help him last time, Person decided to stay in his work clothes. Walker, as usual, was in stylish clothes, as were his aides.

Person began, "Rev. Walker, unless I have been misunderstanding what I read and see, it seems you have some problems with the enterprises at Laughton Park. I am not ashamed of anything we are doing here, so I will answer any general questions you have. I hope you'll forgive me ahead of time for not giving any specific answers about budgets. We are still bidding for projects, and I don't want to tip our hand on anything. Also, I will respect the privacy of workers here, so you can't have any individual salary figures, but I can give you general information. Really, I'm proud of our operation, and I truly hope this meeting will help you understand why."

"Mr. Person, I don't..."

"Mitch. Please call me Mitch," Person interrupted.

This was not the way Walker was used to doing things, but he could adjust. "Mitch, I don't see how you can be proud of an organization that hires African-Americans at below regular wages. This is just like some slave shop."

"For one thing, look about you. It's awfully clean for a slave shop don't you think?" Person was right. The shop was well-kept. The men who worked there respected their machines and kept them clean and in good working order. Because so much sawdust was generated in a day, the workers, Person included, always took the time to clean up after they were done. It wasn't a job that was assigned to the lowest man on the totem pole; it was a responsibility that everybody shared. The two camera men pointed their cameras out the break room windows to capture the work environment.

Person continued, "As far as the wages are concerned, I pay these men as much as I can. It may be below what the ACC pays, but that union gets most of its work through intimidation or legislation. They don't have to compete based on price and quality, so they can pay too much. My companies must be much more competitive. We have to have a low-enough price that some business will risk ACC retaliation to hire a non-union shop."

Good answer, but Walker was not deterred. "You say that, but these African-American brothers and sisters are stuck here. They are in that Catch-22 situation where they can't get a good job with a union wage unless they can get transportation out of this neighborhood, but they can't afford the transportation to get out unless they get a good job with a union wage. Maybe your workers want the union to come in but you won't let it."

"Every one of my employees can afford a car or a bus fare. They can leave if they want to. But the fact is, my workers wouldn't fit in a union shop. They are all independent and, quite frankly, too good."

"These brothers and sisters can't just leave and get a union job if they want to. It will be tough for them because they now have the stigma of working for a non-union shop." Walker felt it was starting to slip away from him. Time to get it back on track.

"Mitch, what would you do if the ACC organized your workers."

"That's simple. I would close shop and move on. But that's a pointless hypothetical situation because it wouldn't happen."

Person had slipped, in Walker's eyes, and the Rev. jumped on it. "If these men and women tried to unionize to improve their working conditions, you would close shop and move on. You see? You are threatening them to accept your lower wages or lose their jobs."

"Rev. Walker, I'm not threatening anybody. My workers know that I would close up if a union forced its way in. I would have to because the joy would be gone from my work. I would rather starve than follow the union rules."

"That's a very selfish attitude."

"Of course it's selfish. That's why I'm here. That's why

we have revitalization in Laughton Park. It's because of selfishness. I'm not doing this to give African-American workers a chance to succeed or because I think this neighborhood needs fixing up. I'm doing this for myself. For my benefit and no one else's. And the workers here are working for their own benefit and selfishness. This place would cease to exist if we started worrying about whether the guy next to us is treated properly or is paid enough. We believe that if a man or woman here feels there is a problem, he or she will take steps to correct it. They aren't going to wait for some union boss to take up their case. They are going to take their case right to the source of the problem, and they will be speaking sincerely, not just whining about some injustice or other, so the problem will be corrected. This is a strong system held together by the invincible bond of an individual's soul to his craft."

"What you are saying describes me. I believe there is a problem, so I am taking my case right to the source, you. I am telling you that you are taking advantage of the disadvantaged. You say when someone takes a sincere problem to the source it will be corrected. Well, here I am. Correct the problem," Walker leaned forward while he was talking. He knew he had created a dramatic moment for the media. He had backed Person into a corner. Now it was time to see what happened.

Person felt helpless. Not because he was in any kind of a tricky PR position, but because he knew this man was too concerned about the reporters and his stature in front of them to really consider anything Person told him. Person always felt helpless whenever he tried to get someone to understand the power and value of individualism if the person could not or would not grasp it.

Finally, Person sighed and said. "Rev. Walker, your soul was abandoned long ago. You can neither understand a real problem nor recognize its solution."

In dramatic fashion, Walker stood up, said some appropriate response and stormed out of the building to answer reporters' questions out on the sidewalk. He gave all the right responses and knew this story was going to come out in his favor. But this was all done in a haze. His mind was clouded by the look Person gave him.

It's true, Walker had not really listened to much of what Person was saying to him through most of their conversation, other than to find a key phrase or two that he could turn to his advantage. But that last statement, accompanied by Person's violating stare, drove the point home hard. He heard every word and felt their meaning.

Had he lost his soul? How was he carrying out his cause? Did he carefully evaluate each situation before him, or did he follow an automated set of activities, honed from years of experience, in an effort to get the best publicity or the most power? Maybe it was time to back off, take a closer look at his goals and see if his methods were helping him get there. What was he really trying to do anyway, get headlines or get equality? Do those always go together?

Those questions haunted Walker throughout a sleepless night. The most troubling part was that he decided he could not change. It was too late. Too many people depended on him to keep the cause in the media and he could not let them down. If he didn't do it, who would? It had to be him. He could not bear the thought of that power going to someone else.

In the morning he felt like he had some answers, but he felt no better.

****

After the evening news, Ron Davis' phone rang. The construction giant picked up the line and recognized Seth Howard's voice on the other end.

"Didn't you love the news tonight," the legislator said. "I'll tell you, that guy just keeps stepping on his dick. Here I am, preparing to release our legislative plans in front of his shop tomorrow and he's on TV tonight giving me a perfect set-up. I couldn't have scripted it better myself."

"You'll have to give Ben Walker a call and thank him."

"He'll be there tomorrow. I'll tell him then. You going to make it?"

"Wouldn't miss it for the world. It sure does seem like we're in a great position for this thing," Davis said.

"You better believe it. I can't believe this Person guy. What the fuck is he thinking? I bet he is the most hated man in Washington City right now. Who can like that guy?"

Davis felt a twang in his gut. He couldn't help thinking

about his daughter. But he kept the conversation going. "Well, you don't score a lot of popularity points by questioning a religious leader's soul on the evening news."

Howard laughed. "Okay, here's an update for you. The bill I'm introducing makes businesses in enterprise zones pay prevailing wage. I think I've got the votes to pass it, but just to hang on to some of the fence sitters, I've included a provision making it clear that those businesses don't have to become union shops."

"That's fine. It's a decent technicality. As long as they pay the prevailing wage, we can compete with them evenly. A bunch of them will become union shops anyway."

"Great. I'll see you tomorrow. Oh, hey, how's this stuff affecting Person's business."

With the help of his PI, Davis had been watching what the negative publicity was doing to Person's pending bids.

"He's getting reamed on the big projects," Davis reported. "Any company of any significant size isn't about to hire him and be pulled into this mess. All his pending bids on big jobs were rejected and a couple of other people won't even accept his bids on upcoming projects."

"Isn't it interesting how this stuff works out? This guy is going to help you increase ACC influence, then he's going to be knocked out of business which will cut your competition. Pretty great, huh?"

Davis' reply had an annoyed tone, not at Howard, but because something had been bugging him. "The thing is, Seth, I don't think we can break him. We got the big prizes out of his hands, but he keeps getting more and more small jobs. Some firms just seem drawn to him, despite this bad publicity. I can't figure it out. He's not going to be able to keep all his current workers, but he won't have to close his doors either."

Howard wasn't aware of that information. It caught him off guard. "Hmm. I wouldn't worry about it, Ron. This thing is still young. We'll see what happens."

TWENTY

Late one evening, Person sat in his office working through his bookkeeping and making some projections. It did not look good. All the big contracts were closed to him, he now realized.

It frustrated him that once businesses became large, they became susceptible to public scrutiny, or more accurately, special interest group extortion. The more powerful and far-reaching a company grew, the more people noticed its success. That made the company a prime target for some group to capitalize on public envy.

Special interest groups always need new issues to stay alive. Frequently, groups form to raise public awareness about one particular issue. Say, for example, a business wants to expand into an old forest. A group of environmentalists may want to preserve that particular forest, so they form a group, collect donations from other concerned people, and organize a campaign to stop the business. If the new group can exert enough pressure, the business may decide, or be forced, to expand elsewhere or not at all.

The new group enjoys a victory and a forest has been

saved. The problem is that the group doesn't disband and the individuals don't go back to their previous lives. No, those people have tasted power, and it ruins them.

They realize that they can play upon the public's envy of a large successful business to bring bad publicity on the business and force that business to do their bidding. Power. Like the lotus eaters, they have no other desire or interest. They look for new forests to save or any issue that is related enough to warrant their interest. And they continue to collect donations.

In fact, the issues they jump on next are determined by the likelihood of those issues bringing in more donations. The focus of the new organization is to become a permanent organization. Why were they created in the first place? To save one particular forest. But that is no longer their drive.

So they are always searching for a new issue, a new battle cry. Do they have the same feeling about the new issue as they did about the original forest? Of course not. Perhaps they wanted to save the original forest because it was near their homes; they grew up playing in the forest; they hunted in the forest for food. It was important to their lives. But once the forest is saved, they decide there are other things worth saving, so they select a river in a different part of the state or nation and work on pushing a local business away from it. How can they care about a river that they have never seen before as deeply as the forest that was a part of their lives? They got involved in saving the forest because they sincerely cared about that forest. They get involved in all the other issues because they sincerely care about remaining in an interest group.

Saving forests and rivers is a worthy cause. But what is the true motivation of that original group? The threshold between a worthy cause and an unworthy quest for power is too easily crossed.

Bigger businesses are better targets for power-hungry groups because those businesses have a public image to maintain, and they probably have enough of a profit margin to adjust their plans or cancel an expansion. The business may have to put off hiring more people or improving its product, but that can be a small price to pay for avoiding a smear campaign directed at its integrity.

Each business that avoids a fight counts as another victory and fuels the fire of the interest group. The group can add another line to its resume to prove its power and use that information to solicit more donations.

Even though Person's Fine Woodworking was not large enough to have a public image to protect, it was a victim of the same kind of campaign launched against mega-corporations. Had the timing been a little different, Person figured, Benham United might well have been the target because it hired the company that had the "unfair" employment practices. Ben Walker and Seth Howard might have gotten even more media attention if they were targeting one of the larger companies in Washington City, rather than Person's upstart construction business.

As it was, things worked out to Benham's advantage and Person's disadvantage. Person guessed that he became the target because he was beginning to encroach on ACC turf. Walker was a pawn in this game, used by Seth Howard and Ron Davis to make Person's life uncomfortable.

Furthermore, because Benham was large and had an established reputation in the city, the public would be less likely to believe the company was trying to re-institute slavery. But Person's Fine Woodworking was an unknown. Walker could exaggerate all he wanted and the public would have no information to the contrary.

Person smiled to himself in frustrated irony as he thought about these events. If his ventures were losing money and his buildings were run down, he would probably be receiving accolades from Walker for hiring minorities. But because he was driven by, and earning, profits he was a criminal. People hate success that is not their own.

He turned his attention back to his books. Recently, he had hired even more Laughton Park African-Americans to work on the Benham United project and the projected new contracts that would be awarded as a result. Now that he was publicly criticized for the way he employed African-Americans, he would not win any of those big contracts, so he would have to *un*employ those same African-Americans.

Not that he was consciously trying to help Laughton Park, but Person couldn't understand how firing these workers was better for them than employing them. He felt bad that good, honest workers were going to be unutilized once again, simply because some loudmouths didn't want Person to utilize their skills for his own profit.

As he was putting together plans for dismissing workers, Willie Bender knocked on his open door.

"Mitch, can I talk for a minute?"

"Come on in. You're here late."

Bender made himself comfortable in a chair across from Person's desk. "I was finishing up my work here."

That caught Person's attention. He sat up a little straighter and looked at the man.

Bender continued. "Mitch, I'm grateful for the opportunity you and the other guys give me here, but I got to move on. I got something else cooking."

Person understood, but he really liked Willie and would not be happy to see him go. "Listen, if you're worried about that meeting with Ben Walker, that wasn't your fault. I know how these things..."

"No, no, no. Nothing to do with that. I felt kinda bad 'bout that though. No, this is something different. It's a chance I can't pass. Anyway, the way I figure, you gonna be letting some people go here soon. If I got something else lined up, I can take it now and maybe somebody else gets to keep working here."

Once again, Person was impressed with Bender's perception. In the short time he had worked for Person, Bender demonstrated an uncanny knack, a sixth sense, for feeling whether profits were down, up, or unchanged. And he usually knew if the change was by a large amount or a small amount, though he couldn't guess exact figures.

A few times, Bender had come to Person or Harry Tom and suggested that profits were slowing in case they wanted to make some schedule adjustments. The men would go back and run some figures and find out that Bender was right.

Person knew that sooner or later, Bender would move on to something better. He was interested in where the man was going, but he knew Bender would tell him if he thought he should know.

"I wish you luck, Willie, though I know you won't need it."

The two shook hands.

As Willie was leaving, Person added, "I'd appreciate it if you don't mention layoffs to anyone else. As soon as I get all the details worked out, I want to let them know, and I'd prefer to do it myself."

"No problem. I'll catch you later."

Not five minutes after Bender left, Sandy came in.

"I want a piece of the action."

Person looked up. And grinned slyly.

"Not that kind of action," she said. Then added with a smile, "at least not right now."

He got serious. "What did you have in mind?"

"I don't have to explain to you that I'm very good at what I do. But I do need to explain that what I do involves you. Unless I am mistaken, you cannot hold on to all your employees very much longer. One of the projects I am working on at my office is an intervention program. When we are able to locate potential layoffs, we want to be on hand to help people with counseling before they receive their last paycheck. We find we can be more effective if we get in touch with people before they are having problems. What can I do for your people, Mitch? They are good, strong men and women. I don't want society to lose them."

"I was just thinking what a waste it would be if these folks were lost to the system," Person said. "It would be an insult to their self-reliance if I made every business decision based on their employment with me, but it would make every day brighter knowing people of their quality were out in the world creating."

He nodded toward the newspaper, which was open to an editorial criticizing the profit motives of Laughton Park. "At times, it seems there are so few of us."

She looked at what he was working on and recognized what it was. "How many have to go?"

"About ten. All the people we hired for Benham United. Right now the smaller projects are still coming in. Actually the number has increased, but that's still only enough to keep the others busy."

"What about the other businesses?"

"They're okay. Right now the focus is on the construction company. The other companies have only been mentioned briefly. I fear they may be next, though."

"When are you going to break the news to your people?"

"Looks like tomorrow."

"Can I be on hand."

"Normally I would say no. These workers are strong people. They have confidence in themselves and a devotion to leaving the mark of quality wherever they go. It would be an insult to them to think they need a social worker to make a go of it. On the other hand, I know you. You don't treat them like they need you."

"They don't need me. But I have information that they can use. Face it, these men and women are African-Americans. They are not treated the same as you and me. They don't always have the same opportunities that other people do. Unfortunately, racism still exists and sometimes it keeps African-Americans from having access to information on jobs and opportunities. I'm trying to keep the information flowing to everybody who can use it. They don't need me, but that doesn't mean I don't have something to offer."

"Yeah, why don't you come by tomorrow afternoon and do what you can. I think my employees respect you. Do you have any leads?"

"I'm working on something right now. It could pan out."

Person kept an open door policy for his office. He figured he didn't have anything to hide from his employees, so his door was always open during meetings, bookkeeping, or other jobs that he performed in his office. It was never a problem because people trusted him and he trusted them. They didn't feel the need to snoop or anything else. If he had something important to tell them, he would. If they wanted to share something with him, or if they had a concern about something he was working on, they felt comfortable going in.

Though he never closed the door, right now he was glad he had not removed it. When his conversation with Sandy wore down he went to the door, kicked a few boxes out of its way, and closed it. Knowing his open door policy, any employees who came in late would understand that if the door was closed there was a good reason for it. The couple would not be disturbed.

Once again, they lost themselves to the world. When they were not making love, they could talk and discuss business with complete civility. They would not abandon their professional conversation until they had thoroughly covered the topic. At that point, the switch was thrown and they became objects driven by passion. Business, Laughton Park, social work; those things were part of some other place. That was the place where individuality and selfishness were the diving driving force. Lovemaking took them to a new world. Here, the fiercest individuals were committed to becoming a single animal with two souls.

TWENTY-ONE

Seth Howard's news conference in front of Person's Fine Woodworking went well. He stood at a podium on the sidewalk, holding a draft of his new "Fair Wage" legislation, flanked by Rev. Walker, Ron Davis, and a few legislators who wanted in on the action.

The name "Fair Wage" had been chosen because it helped tie the legislation, which was primarily a union tool, to the civil rights issue. Besides, the term "prevailing wage" automatically made some opposition legislators and conservative members of the public get defensive. The Fair Wage name didn't really fool any lawmakers, but it was a little more palatable. And for the general apathetic public, it was easier to support something "fair" than something "prevailing."

Howard had fun with bills like these. He knew some legislators were going to oppose this bill because they did not believe in government-imposed wages. By tying the prevailing wage bill to a civil rights bill, he was going to give those people headaches when they had to go back to their districts and explain why they voted against civil rights, especially "fair" civil rights.

Many of those lawmakers on the other side of the political aisle were in safe districts. Howard's tactics would only serve as an annoyance to them. But a few of the districts were only marginally safe, which meant this "headache" could help sway independent voters to Howard's party during the next election.

The interesting thing about political divisions in the legislature was that the real battle was below the surface of what was portrayed to the public. Republicans and Democrats would take philosophical sides of an issue and battle it out in legislative chambers and on the campaign trail. The rhetoric would fly during stump speeches and ensuing news reports. However, the real fight was rarely philosophical. Rather, it was was a public relations battle to set up a few key legislative votes that might sway a handful of voters in a few select districts.

Entire bills were written with the sole intent of forcing one or two lawmakers into an embarassing vote that might cost him an election. The author of the bill cared little about the legislation itself. The battle for the majority of seats in the legislative chamber reigned supreme.

In virtually every legislative body, only about 10 percent of the seats are real electoral contests. The rest of the seats are safe -- assuming the incumbent doesn't get caught with the altar boy. Political ringmasters like Howard plan and scheme throughout the legislative session conjuring ways to force votes on issues that might sway one or two of those electoral contests to their party. The more successful he or she (usually he) is at winning those elections, the more likely his colleagues will continue to choose him as their leader.

Howard was a master at finding issues to affect vulnerable districts. A subtle change like "prevailing" to "fair" would not by itself determine an election, but compounded with other plans he intended to carry out, the maneuver would move him one step closer to winning another legislative seat for his party.

His news conference was well covered. As usual, the employees of Person's Fine Woodworking were out at various job sites, so no one was available for an immediate response. Person was interrupted the rest of the day by the ringing of his cellular phone. He was even less interested in responding this time than he was after the last news conference.

Most of the media gave the story good coverage. The legislative session would be starting in a few days, and this was a good issue to kick off all the legislative preview stories. To tell the story, reporters had to rehash the events at Laughton Park, but for the most part, the story angle changed from a Laughton Park story to a legislative story. The tone of most coverage was similar to the story that ran in the *Times-Union*:

Laughton Park to be Target
of Fair Wage Bill

by Aaron Teldon

Washington City -- Keeping his promise to close a civil rights loophole in the Laughton Park area of the city, state Rep. Seth Howard of Washington City today proposed legislation that would require all businesses located in enterprise zones to pay a "fair wage" to their employees.

The issue arose when Howard discovered that a local businessman was making large profits by hiring only minority workers and paying them below union scale for their labor. The company, Person's Fine Woodworking, has since been the target of several protests by the city's Act Now organization and the Associated Council of Carpenters.

Although Person's Fine Woodworking has broken no specific civil rights laws, the company's employment practices have drawn fire because the firm benefits from enterprise zone tax breaks.

"It's bad enough that this company is taking advantage of underprivileged African-American workers, but you add that to the fact that the company does this while paying less than its fair share of property taxes and you have a real monster in the heart of Washington City," said Howard.

"The legislation I hold in my hand is the stake we will drive into the heart of this monster," he added as he stood in front of Person's Fine Woodworking, waving the legislation he will introduce when the legislature reconvenes next week.

Nicknamed the "Fair Wage" bill, Howard's legislation would require any company that receives tax breaks from enterprise zones or other economic development agreements to pay its employees a "fair wage." The fair wage would match the prevailing wage, determined by area union contracts.

Howard explained that the legislation is needed to close a loophole that allows a company to receive tax breaks and pay its workers below union scale. The tax breaks were created to lure businesses to blighted areas. But companies like Person's Fine Woodworking have taken advantage of the system, he said.

"They get a double advantage by having tax breaks and by slashing their labor costs. They exploit local workers who may not be able to afford transportation to other jobs. That gives the company an unfair advantage over other businesses that choose to pay their workers fairly.

This is just a fair business competition bill," Howard said.

Rev. Benjamin Walker, leader of the city's Act Now organization, said the legislation is necessary to "stop the slave-labor conditions in Laughton Park."

When contacted for comment, company owner Mitchell Person said, "My construction company will remain in operation only as long as it is profitable. It was created as a profitable business, not as a charitable organization."

He would not elaborate on the meaning of his comments, but Howard speculated that Person was using a scare tactic to threaten the loss of jobs in Laughton Park in an effort to stop the Fair Wage bill.

The story ran next to a photo of Howard holding up his legislation while Davis, Walker and the others applauded.

The *Endurance* came out the next day. Its story took a different tone:

The Laughton Park Circus:
Who are the Real Clowns?

by Sam Janus

Washington City -- With joyful self-righteousness, the state's media have been reporting on a supposedly dastardly business development in one of the city's hell-holes, otherwise known as Laughton Park.

As usual, the other media are reporting only the part of the story that is hand-fed to them by Rep. Seth Howard and his gang of goons. Readers of the *Endurance* know that any story involving Seth Howard -- until we finally get to report that he's been indicted for something -- should be treated with caution. The Laughton Park story is yet one more example.

First, their story: Local businessman Mitchell Person opens a construction company in an enterprise zone in Laughton Park. Because of its location, he gets property tax breaks. Then he hires minorities from the local neighborhood because he knows they're so damn happy to finally have a job that they won't complain if he pays them below union scale. Due to the tax breaks he receives and the low wages he pays, he is sitting on a huge pile of money. He buys up other buildings in the enterprise zone and continues the low wages, making him a zillionaire while the poor minorities have barely enough money to get by.

Sounds awful doesn't it. Hard to believe that kind of thing could happen in this day and age.

Well, it *should* be hard to believe. It's a bunch of crap.

Not willing to accept Howard's rhetoric, this paper investigated the Laughton Park activities, found a good source, and now we have the real story:

The salaries: It's true the workers in Laughton Park are earning below union scale, but they're not exactly making minimum wage either. They are skilled craftsmen and, accordingly, they are making more than they would in any unskilled job. But the union scale is so out of touch with the job market that nobody outside the ACC's sphere of influence can afford to pay it.

To protect the privacy of the Laughton Park workers, our source asked us not to reveal actual numbers. We'll honor that. But we did some calculations and discovered that if Mitchell Person suddenly started paying union scale and allowed the ACC to infiltrate his business, the increased salary for each worker would barely cover union dues and higher tax burdens.

The union: If unionized construction companies had to compete with non-union shops on a level playing field, the union groups would never win because they cost so much. That's why the ACC and its chief goon, Ron Davis, work so hard to make sure the playing field is not level. They've got laws, most introduced by Seth Howard, that give them advantages in all contracts that involve public money. If the laws don't work, they have intimidation.

Union tactics have kept most non-union shops in the small time where they can't take big projects away from ACC companies. Recently, however, the big Benham United renovation bid went to a non-union shop...Person's Fine Woodworking, located in Laughton Park.

Act Now: Once again, Act Now boss Rev. Ben Walker is fighting the right battle on the wrong battlefield. Our snooping around determined that he was not brought into this by any complaints from the people working in Laughton Park. His involvement came after Seth Howard brought the media into it. Walker is so interested in headlines that he doesn't do his homework anymore. He just says what he knows will play on the evening news.

Is he still performing a service for his constituency? Will Laughton Park be better off if Person is chased out and the workers find themselves unemployed again?

Seth Howard: It's apparent this man has never had any integrity. So why does he still hold office and why does the media still spread his ideas like fresh manure on a garden? He's now introducing legislation to "correct the problem" in Laughton Park. It would require businesses in enterprise zones to pay union scale. Isn't the ACC the largest contributor to his personal campaign account and also the House Victory Campaign Committee account, which he controls?

If you haven't figured out the true story of Laughton Park yet, back up a few paragraphs and re-read the union section.

<u>Mitchell Person</u>: Person is the enigmatic piece of this situation. We have figured out the motivations of all the people involved, except him. Perhaps his biggest problem is that he says he is involved in this business venture for his own benefit. He doesn't even pretend that he is being charitable. Such selfishness, no matter how sincere, rarely gets good headlines.

Maybe it's time we re-think how we view selfishness. If someone says he is doing something from the bottom of his heart or merely to help others, we the cynical public have learned that he is probably really acting for himself. But if somebody skips the crap and says he is doing it for himself, we act incensed. For some reason, we prefer the lie.

Though Person is admittedly selfish, it is not the kind of selfishness we are used to. He is not chasing material things that other rich people have (we drove by his apartment, and believe us, you wouldn't want to live there). Instead, his selfishness is focused on constructing things the way he thinks they should be constructed. He does not maximize profits at the expense of quality. If he cut a few corners, perhaps he could pay his workers more, but the projects would not be up to his selfish standard.

The odd thing is, all his workers that we met share the same dedication to selfish accomplishment. It's a wonder that they can work together at all, but they work together beautifully. They work like a precision machine lubricated by respect and fueled by the desire for quality.

<u>What happens next?</u>: Person has hinted that he will close shop once the joy and the profit are taken out. Some of the controversy instigators say he's bluffing, but we believe otherwise. We predict Howard's bill will pass, Person will go out of business, and Laughton Park will return to its former miserable state.

Stay tuned.

The *Endurance* also carried a photograph of Howard's news conference. They weren't invited to the conference, but Janus found out about it in time to grab a camera and go. His photograph, in usual *Endurance* style, was not the set up planned by Howard. Instead, it was from behind the podium, showing Howard and his entourage facing a bunch of reporters who were hanging on his every word.

TWENTY-TWO

Ron Davis walked through Seth Howard's outer office, past all the staffers who were busily assembling packets of newspaper articles about Laughton Park. The plan was to put together a packet of articles, from newspapers throughout the state, criticizing the businesses in Laughton Park and praising Seth Howard's legislation. Those packets would be placed on the desks of all the legislators right before the day's legislative session began. It was one of Howard's little lobbying techniques.

Not surprisingly, the *Endurance* article was not included in the packet.

It was, however, in Davis' briefcase as he went back to Howard's office. Like many influential people in town, Davis read the alternative paper, but didn't want anybody to know he read it.

Once Howard's door was closed, Davis removed the article from his briefcase.

"Did you see this piece of shit?" he asked, thrusting the clipping toward his friend. "God, I hate that paper."

Howard laughed. He had seen it earlier that day, so he

didn't accept Davis' offering. He walked back to his desk and sat down. Davis did the same.

"I'm always amazed at how accurate he is," the legislator said.

"How can you sit there so calmly? He didn't exactly treat you like a saint."

"He never does. But look where I am and look where he is. I am in control of the state legislature and he is in control of a small newspaper. If he mattered at all, would I still be here? Would you? He may have an uncanny knack for hitting the target, but his weapon is too small to hurt anybody."

"But it can't help you to have this kind of shit about you in print."

"Actually, it does help me. The fact that his criticisms bounce off me sends a subtle message to other lawmakers that their criticisms might bounce off me too."

"Well, I'd like to get even. I don't like his shit and I think it's time to let him know. And I don't mean with some friendly phone call."

"No!" Howard threw Davis a serious look. "The minute you do something to him, you give him credibility. Right now people may read this and chuckle, but they think he's a crackpot. Even if they believe him, they don't do anything about it, because he's not part of the mainstream media. If something happens to him, then he, and what he says, gets covered by the real press. Then you'll have problems.

"If you want reporters to turn on you with a fury that

you've never seen, just threaten their freedom of the press and make a martyr out of one of their own. The other reporters don't like Janus, but they support his right to be a reporter."

Davis didn't respond. No sense fighting with Howard today, but there would be other days. Janus would not get by without retaliation from him, he thought. Turning to other matters, Davis reached into his briefcase and pulled out a sizeable check. He handed it to Howard.

"That should get this legislation moving," he said.

"Thank you Ron, the House Victory Campaign Committee appreciates your support," Howard smiled.

"How's the count?"

"I haven't started pushing yet, but I count an easy 45 votes today. We've got about ten leaning our way and probably another five to ten that are undecided. I think you can figure an easy 60 votes by the time this comes to the floor. I'd like to send it to the Senate with as big a message behind it as possible. When a couple of the fence-sitters see this check in the campaign account, they'll start salivating and doing anything they can to get a piece of it."

Howard only needed 51 votes to pass a bill through the 100-member House of Representatives. Once a bill was passed by the House, it was sent to the Senate, where Howard had little control. At least directly. If the House passed the bill with a large-enough majority, Senators would understand that Howard controlled a solid block of votes. One that could kill a Senator's pet project if that Senator balked at the Fair Wage bill.

Howard felt good about his legislation. Starting with 45 solid votes before he even started pushing! He told Davis 60 votes, but Howard was confident he could line up more than 70.

The men talked for a while and Howard got up and started organizing his papers for the day's session. The staff had already left to distribute the news clippings. Victory was in the air.

****

"I think it's time to unload them." Harry Tom sat in the break room looking at the other members of the management team.

"I don't think they're ready," Ramsey said. "I don't think we can get out of them what they're worth, and even if we sell them now, I don't think they are established enough to make the payments to us."

Elders jumped in. "But if we don't sell them now, they won't be worth shit in another couple of weeks. Then we lose everything."

In the break room, the men were discussing the negative publicity and the resulting layoffs at Person's construction company. Person was annoyed that they were wasting time worrying about the actions of other people, namely the reporters and policymakers who were involved in the situation. But Harry Tom pointed out to him that if the events started bleeding over to the other Laughton Park businesses, then they all stood to lose money, not just Person. Mitch acknowledged the point, and the discussion continued.

According to their original plans, the investors would have sold the companies to their executive managers over the next five years. By that time, those companies would have proven that they would either sink or swim. The swimmers could afford to pay off Person and friends to gain full ownership. The investors didn't want to sell the businesses too early, because profitable businesses would do more for the property values than marginal businesses. That was, after all, the reason they started expanding in the first place.

Now, however, they were in the situation they all detested. Having their hand forced by someone else, for reasons other than creation.

"I wouldn't mind selling now, even though it's early, but where are these managers going to get the money? Where's LaRon Dempsey going to find the cash to buy his painting company?" asked Niles.

"That's what banks are for," said Niles.

"Bullshit," responded Elders. "Maybe you could go in the bank and get a loan, but you're a white guy who used to be a lawyer. Dempsey is a Black man who was unemployed for a long time before he hooked up with us. No bank is going to have as much faith in his management skills as we do."

The point was a good one. Elders was not one to throw around charges of racism casually. If he said African-Americans had a disadvantage in some situations, they believed him.

"Aren't there some special minority loan programs through the state Department of Commerce?" Thomas asked.

"Sure there are. And that section is headed up by a guy who owes his job to our good friend Seth Howard," said Niles.

They were quiet as they contemplated other options.

"Where did Willie Bender go? If he started something on his own, didn't he need some capital?" asked Ramsey.

"You know, he never did tell me what he is starting," said Person. "I figured it was his business so I never asked him. I'm real curious now. All I know is that he worked with Sandy a little bit."

Around the table, people stopped talking. They just looked at Person, waiting.

"I guess I better call then," he said. They nodded.

He went to the wall phone in the break room and called. After brief greeting, he explained that he wanted to know where Willie Bender was. Bender had not left a number.

"Mitch, I keep my work with people confidential. I won't even tell you."

"I respect that, but we might need you to do the same thing, whatever it was, for some other folks." He went on to explain their dilemma.

"Tell you what, get the executive managers together tomorrow night and I'll talk with them. You guys can be there too."

With that set, the meeting broke up and the men went out to Miller's Tavern for a beer.

During the evening, Travis asked Person what he thought of the article in the *Endurance*.

"It's funny how I'm involved in this thing, yet I couldn't see what is going on as well as Janus did."

"Part of the reason is that you are not concerned about people's motivations. To you, people are either good, bad or confused. Once you decide which, you don't care much what they do. You figure their actions will be an extension of their goodness, badness or confusion. On the other hand, Sam is almost obsessed with people's motivations. He believes, and rightly so, that people are constantly trying to hide their real motivations for doing things. He wants to cut through the crap and know exactly why people are really doing what they are doing.

"You're concerned with *what* people do. You think their final actions clearly demonstrate who they are. He is concerned with *why* they do it. He thinks their intricate actions demonstrate who they are."

"Which of us is correct?" Person grinned at his friend.

"Both, neither. I don't really know. I think you make a quick but accurate judgement about someone and don't concern yourself with their actions if they do not have a strong self. When Sam sees that someone is bad or confused, he feels a need to point it out and scream it as loud as he can. It really bugs him that the insecure and the morally vacant are running the show."

"He's an interesting guy, Travis. I'm glad you introduced me to him."

The men redirected their conversation to woodworking.

When the men got together outside of the office, they did not talk about the business end of woodworking and construction. They talked about the actual hands-on shaping and joining of wood. The feel, the smell, the sense of accomplishment. The real reason behind the business.

As the gathering was breaking up for the night, Travis leaned over to Person. "He's wrong you know."

"Yeah. But that's okay." Even without explanation, Person knew Niles was talking about Janus.

Niles continued. "They aren't really running the show. They're only running *their* show. They can't affect what we do unless we let them. They might be able to change the setting or the scenery, but that's only superficial stuff."

"Well said."

The two men walked out into the night.

TWENTY-THREE

In the House Labor Committee, lawmakers discussed the Fair Wage bill and then passed it unanimously. Howard had delivered a brief outline of the legislation, then turned the floor over to Rev. Walker for a colorful description of the injustice that caused a need for the bill.

The room was packed with media who didn't want to miss the first significant legislative action on the bill. Under normal circumstances, Howard would find a victimized citizen to testify in favor of his legislation. Such testimony made for great TV. But neither he nor Walker could find any Laughton Park workers who were interested in testifying in favor of the bill. None of the media seemed to notice the lack of first-hand testimony.

Against the bill, the Chamber of Commerce testified that the bill would essentially increase the cost of doing business in the many enterprise zones throughout the state. They reminded the committee that the enterprise zones were created because business needed tax incentives to lure them to otherwise undesirable parts of the city. If labor costs were forced to rise, they argued, the tax breaks would not be enough to keep existing companies in enterprise zones or to attract new industries.

The Chamber was stuck. They did not want to appear insensitive to the race issue, but they saw that Howard was merely using race to mask his pro-labor bill. They had to fight it, but couldn't figure out a tactful method. In their meetings, the Chamber executives cursed Mitchell Person, who they had never met, for putting them in this situation.

During his testimony, the Chamber lobbyist proposed an amendment that would go along with Fair Wages, but grant an even larger enterprise zone tax break to counteract possible negative effects.

Howard gave a hard look to his loyal followers on the committee, and the proposal was soundly defeated.

Anticipating such maneuvers by the Chamber, Howard made sure the Speaker assigned his bill to the Labor Committee instead of the Commerce Committee. He was certain the bill would pass either committee, but he wanted a unanimous vote, with no significant amendments, and he did not have the same control over the Commerce Committee as he did the Labor Committee.

For one, Howard was chairman of the Labor Committee. Also, he had concentrated on making sure the membership of that committee was in his court. He could muscle the Commerce Committee too, but there were a few unpredictable lawmakers serving there.

A couple of legislators from the other party supported the amendment, but he knew those votes were to help placate their pro-business constituency. Their votes would be with him to pass the amendment-less bill out of committee.

****

In her years with the state human services agency, Sandy had worked through some tough problems. She viewed her job as a way to help needy citizens find a way to get out of the welfare system. In so doing, she had become an expert at running into all the bureaucratic roadblocks, and working around them.

The first problem was the old, yet seemingly immortal, race issue. Because the majority of her clients were minorities, she found in trying to help them many of the same problems they encountered every day. Employers who were unwilling to hire skilled African-Americans into skilled jobs; neighborhoods that were, for all practical purposes, closed to African-American residents. In fact, she felt she was as close to knowing how racism feels as is possible for any white woman. Yet through persistence, she was able to find many decent employment opportunities for her minority clients.

Another problem she frequently encountered was with the system that was supposed to help her clients. The welfare system, tinkered with during every legislative session, was a tangled mess of rules and regulations that contradicted themselves, if not the very goals of the agency. Through time, the agency and its rules had become so massive that it was impossible to come in and "fix" them. Therefore, complaints of inefficiency and fraud only led to more tinkering, which merely exacerbated the problem.

Sometimes, she suspected that the agency had long abandoned its goal of helping people get back into society and instead was more determined to perpetuate the need for its services. She saw the inherent problem with an agency that, in a perfect world, would eventually eliminate the need for itself if it worked properly.

Bureaucracies, like organisms, are in a constant struggle to survive. But rather than chasing antelope on an African plain, bureaucracies chase the public dollar on the legislative plain. When the antelope are scarce, the battle between lions, hyenas and other carnivores becomes fierce. When public dollars are scarce, the legislative battles between bureaucracies and special interest groups becomes equally fierce. If the legislative "gods" provide more public dollars, then there is less violence, but the gods are reluctant to answer the prayers of the hungry bureaucracies and interest groups. Besides, the more dollars that roam the plain, the more species appear to eat them.

Sandy didn't believe that anybody in her agency actually wanted needy people to stay needy. Virtually everyone she met in her massive agency was good-hearted. But all were easily distracted by turf wars, office politics and other matters that didn't really relate to helping people get off welfare. It hadn't occurred to any of them, she thought, that the agency ought to be finding a way to get society to the point where the agency's role, and size, would be minimal. No, they were all caught up in keeping the organism alive and growing.

The challenge of facing the institutional attitude of self-preservation is that the institution is rarely receptive to changes. As Sandy would run into conflicting rules or duplications and inefficiencies, she would try to clean up the process or find a way around the problem. But each rule for the agency had a person attached to it, someone who thought it was necessary in the first place. She angered a lot of co-workers who felt she was "out to get them" or that she was stepping on their toes. Their insecurities didn't dissuade her, but she learned to be more cautious of her co-worker's feelings.

But the most frustrating part of her job was not that the roadblocks existed, but that some of her clients had no interest in working with her to get around them. So many people had given up, had lost hope.

Of course there were people who cheated the system, though not nearly as many as conservative rhetoric would lead people to believe. The confusing mass of regulations made it nearly impossible not to break some rules. Broken rules were due more to ignorance or misguided rules than fraud. But a few people were really trying to "win" the welfare game.

Those people caused Sandy much despair. They will never "win" the game as long as they are dependent on it, she thought. Each time a person would figure out a way to squeeze a few more undeserved dollars out of the system, he would become more and more addicted to dependence on someone else. He might be a few dollars ahead, but the price was that he put off a chance to get hundreds of dollars ahead. It is like a drunk who runs out of money in a tavern but keeps bumming drinks off other customers. He thinks he is being clever, but he is only feeding the disease that keeps him from success.

To the frauds, Sandy was harsh. As she would work the rules to help the many clients who wanted to be self-sufficient, she could also work the rules to severely punish the few who wanted to be dependent. She really didn't think it would change them, but she thought it was worth the chance.

The key to Sandy's success with clients was that she did not view herself as an extension of the benevolent state. She did not approach her clients with the air of one who controls the purse strings, therefore their lives.

Instead of discussions with clients about what they were and were not eligible for, Sandy worked with them to find out where they were going and then figured out how to get them what was available to help them reach their goals. Her clients then felt that the state aid was merely an extension of their own ability to earn. The results were remarkable.

Currently, her personal challenge was that her clients all taste the glorious nectar of self-actualization. A few men and women who had, until recently, worked for Mitchell Person, had touched their own egos, and were not about to settle for satisfying someone else's desires or purposes. They would not work for a union where individuality and creativity were killed for the sake of solidarity and structure.

Quite frankly, the welfare system was not set up to handle people like Mitch's former employees, because they usually made good on their own. The problem here was that the men and women were minorities from a poor background, so their willingness to succeed would butt up against financial disadvantages and ignorant racism.

They had earned some money, but did not have enough capital to buy their businesses. Getting a loan would be nearly impossible. Since they would not work for just "any" shop, Sandy would have her hands full giving them options. Not that they asked for or even expected her help, but she liked these people and wanted to give them whatever information they could use.

Technically, she should not have been helping them at all. They were not part of her caseload, nor would they qualify for public assistance. But she viewed her job as multifaceted. If she could help them, then she should.

Recently, she had stumbled across a program that, again technically, she should not have been working on. It didn't fit into her job description as her supervisor viewed it, but it fit into her principles. That was good enough. Besides, she tried to work on it mostly during non-office hours.

It was a challenge, but she enjoyed it.

TWENTY-FOUR

Laughton Park Companies Sold

by Aaron Teldon

Washington City -- Local business developer Mitchell Person has sold his interests in all companies operating in Laughton Park, it was announced today. Some observers say the pressures and lost business from alleged racist business practices forced him out.

For the past week, business and community leaders have speculated that Person and his investors would sell the variety of Laughton Park businesses to the managers of those firms. This morning, it played out as expected. Now those companies are owned and operated by minorities.

In a surprise move, Person also sold his own company, Person's Fine Woodworking to an unidentified group of investors.

"Maybe he felt guilty because of his racist ideas. Maybe he found that no one wanted to do business with him and his racist activities. Either way, I claim this as a victory for Act Now and for the African-Americans who are now rightful owners of these fine companies," said Rev. Benjamin Walker, leader of the Washington City Act Now organization.

Walker acknowledged that he did not expect Person to sell his own construction company, but that it was a "pleasant surprise that further sweetened this victory in our ongoing struggle for equality."

Two months ago, Person came under fire for paying his minority workforce below union scale. Act Now and representatives from the Associated Council of Carpenters protested his business, claiming he was taking advantage of needy minorities. The situation was further fueled by the fact that Person's businesses were in the Laughton Park enterprise zone, enabling Person to benefit from property tax breaks.

The controversy led state Rep. Seth Howard of Washington City to introduce legislation requiring all businesses receiving enterprise zone tax breaks to pay workers a "fair wage" based on the union scale. Howard was more skeptical of Person's actions.

"I think Mr. Person sold these businesses, including his own, to try and stall the Fair Wage bill. But his plan will backfire, because his action demonstrates that even the threat of a Fair Wage law will force bigots out of our enterprise zones," said Howard.

Howard's Fair Wage bill was unanimously passed by

committee a week ago, and yesterday survived a second reading in the House with no amendments. Howard says he has enough votes lined up for the bill to sail through final reading in the House and on to the Senate for further consideration.

LaRon Dempsey is the new owner of True Colors Painting, formerly owned by Person and his investors.

His thoughts on the situation were mixed.

"Of course I'm thrilled to be running my own business. It's a dream come true. But I'm sorry to see Mitch go. This chance wouldn't have come along if it weren't for him," Dempsey said.

Person was unavailable for comment.

****

Person reported for work at the company he owned until two days ago. According to the purchase agreement between him and his buyers, he would still be in charge of operations until he finished the projects started before the sale. He would leave once the projects were completed. Another stipulation was that his name no longer be associated with the company.

He planned to finish by the end of the week. So far, all the construction employees were still on hand, making sure the projects would be finished. The new owners told them their jobs were safe, despite the change in command.

Person was loading his tools on his truck before heading out to a job site, when he stopped to talk to LaRon Dempsey. Ironically, the new owners hired Dempsey to paint the new sign for the construction company, whenever they decided what the new name would be. As a gesture to his old boss, Dempsey had come early to paint over Person's name, leaving the sign blank until he got further orders. He was still on his ladder when Person approached him.

Dempsey climbed down and the two men talked for a few minutes. Suddenly, Rudy Jefferson ran out of his print shop toward them. His eyes were wide open as if in shock.

"Mitch, those guys who bought your place just sold it again. I heard it on the radio just now. You ain't gonna believe who bought it."

The two men didn't say anything. They waited.

"Ron Davis," Jefferson said.

Dempsey was shocked too. He and Jefferson just stared at Person.

"Well...There goes the neighborhood," Person said as he walked toward his truck.

When Person drove off, Dempsey turned to Jefferson. "He's smooth. He's gotta feel like dirt about now, but he hid it well."

"He may not feel that bad, 'cause he'll be the hell out of here. Look at me, I'm gonna be neighbors with that Davis asshole."

****

"What do you mean nobody's there?" Ron Davis was on the phone with the supervisor he had sent to manage the new Laughton Park Construction company he had owned for a week. He was disgruntled to find that the new company he bought had no contracts lined up. Person finished those projects that had been started already, but all other clients for whom work had not started yet, cancelled their contracts. It had taken him a week to reschedule some projects from Davis Construction so his new company would have something to do.

He lined up a few contracts and expected them to be started today. Yesterday, he sent his supervisor over to meet with the crew and explain the new management system and the details of union membership.

"I thought they were looking at me kind of funny yesterday," the supervisor said. "But I just figured that's the way Black folks are. Then I came in today and the place was empty. At first I thought they was late, but here it's 10:00 and nobody's come in."

"Where the hell are they?" Davis was furious.

"I don't know boss. They just aren't here."

"Have any of them filled out their union cards yet?"

"No. They ain't done nothing."

"Good, then they're fired. Just lock the doors and get your ass back here. I'll figure something out. But first, go by the

Wentler site and the Sandco site and get some guys. Take them out to Rendel Industries to get started on what those Laughton Park guys were supposed to do today."

He hung up and sat back, cursing. Then he buzzed his PR man. While he was waiting he reevaluated the Laughton Park deal. He had been approached by a local business developers' group to purchase Person's construction company and the nearby buildings. He had been thinking about buying it anyway, because he had had much success buying out competitors in the past. This group had beaten him to it, but he figured they saw they would not be able to compete with Davis Construction, so they wanted to sell it to Davis himself.

Davis was pretty good at figuring out who got what in business deals. He figured Person made some, but not a lot of, money off his original investment, but that was okay because he had undertaken all the physical renovation. Person would continue to make money on the deal because he would still be paid off, with interest, for the businesses he sold to the Blacks. Davis, however, would collect money from the Blacks too because he now owned the buildings that housed their companies. They would pay him rent for a long time.

He thought the developers probably made a small profit off the deal too. Not much more than a typical middle-man makes. Besides, their price was fair.

Davis' profits would come in the long run. His PR man had convinced him that buying the Laughton Park shops would boost his and the union's image. Given the racial problems caused by the company's previous owner, Davis could look like a savior riding in to end the oppression in Laughton Park. Besides, this company would allow him to target smaller contracts more efficiently. And since his new company would continue to receive a tax break, he could try to undercut many of his smaller, non-union competitors.

Unfortunately, things were not running as smoothly as he expected. When the PR secretary came in, Davis whirled around in his chair and glared at him.

"The public relations benefits of owning a minority-run outfit only exist if minorities actually work there," Davis said. He then explained that apparently the entire staff of Laughton Park Construction quit.

The PR man sat for a moment. He did not ruffle easily, even when his boss was mad at him. Davis respected that, but it also irritated him.

Finally, the PR secretary responded. "Actually, this may be better than we planned." He explained his idea.

The guy earned his salary, thought Davis as he listened to the plan. The man still irritated him though.

****

Once again, Ron Davis, Seth Howard and Benjamin Walker stood on the sidewalk in Laughton Park, in front of a construction company, holding court before a crowd of reporters.

By now the reporters were starting to grumble, especially the newspaper and radio reporters who did not rely on pictures to get their story out. They told Howard's press secretary to start picking a nicer location if he wanted them to keep showing up.

The press secretary knew, however, that they would keep showing as long as Howard could keep the meetings newsworthy. Today's conference was significant news. The reporters would be satisfied with today's feeding.

Ron Davis started the show this time. "Thank you for coming today. We are here to announce an innovative program designed to cure the disease that so recently infected this business district. We are ready to announce new hope for the proud citizens of Laughton Park.

"As many of you know, my company recently purchased this infamous construction company. We did this to show the city that minority men and women can work at a skilled trade and earn a fair union wage.

"So today, I am officially announcing the opening of the Laughton Park Construction Company." Applause broke out among the crowd that the ACC and Act Now had assembled.

Davis continued, "My first action for my new venture is to post this." He held aloft a sign that said "Now Hiring." More applause.

It was Howard's turn. "I want to congratulate Ron Davis on his bold venture. His gracious endeavor comes at the same time my Fair Wage legislation is sailing through the state legislature. His company will be a sign for all other companies in the state to set aside their greedy, selfish motives and give our inner-city residents a fair opportunity at a fair salary."

Now, Walker took the microphone. "This is a proud day for the African-American men and women in our community. We have repelled the invasion of racism and God has smiled on us by bringing in new jobs and new hope.

"Once, this block was controlled by a selfish man who cared only about profit. Now look. These businesses are owned by proud African-American men. The construction company is owned by a man who will give all African-Americans a chance to apply, not just those who are willing to work for a substandard wage. This is a bright day in Laughton Park."

Applause broke out again, but quickly subsided so the reporters could ask questions.

One reporter, who was clearly cynical, asked, "What happened to the minorities who were already employed here? Are they going to be replaced or what?"

"No. Of course not. We will give them every opportunity to be our first employees," Davis responded. It wasn't really a lie, though not the full truth either. He felt no need to inform the reporters that the previous workers all quit.

"Mr. Davis, how should somebody apply?" asked one of the TV reporters.

"Monday morning we will begin accepting applications. Anyone who wants to apply is welcome. Initially, we plan on hiring only 25 people. We realize that's not very many considering the number of people in this neighborhood who would like a job. But we hope to expand as quickly as possible."

It was Aaron Teldon's turn. "Won't it be difficult to make a profit at first? How do you intend to keep this business afloat?"

Seemingly an innocent question, but it had been planted by one of Howard's staffers. Davis paused for dramatic effect, then stared directly at the crowd.

"Unlike the man here before me, my motive is not profit," he began. "I feel the people in this neighborhood have been overlooked for too long. They deserve good-paying jobs. My other construction company is healthy enough that I will not starve if this new business loses money the first few years. Whether I get rich is not important to me. I am not trying to get rich. I only want the residents of Laughton Park to have a chance.

"You see, the philosophy will be different than it was before. We will not throw away applicants simply because those people want a fair job with fair benefits. We won't have a narrow criteria for determining who is acceptable. If you want a job, you have a right to one. That is enough for us.

"We have an obligation to help the people of this community. That is what we are here to do, whether it is profitable or not."

Teldon had a follow up. "Representative Howard, how will this action affect your Fair Wage bill? It's scheduled for a Senate committee hearing tomorrow."

"Good question." Of course it was. Howard's staff had given it to him. "I think Mr. Davis' selfless actions will provide the coattails to carry my bill through the Senate. Mr. Davis is demonstrating that fair wages are fair to both the worker and the employer. There is no economic hardship in fighting racism."

A few clean-up questions were asked by various reporters. Then the news conference ended.

Picture-wise, the scene for this news conference was much like that of the other news conferences and demonstrations. The day's celebrities posed in front of the backdrop made up of the renovated construction company. There were two major differences.

The first change was obvious. Instead of the "Person's Fine Woodworking" sign above the door, the sign read "Laughton Park Construction Company." Davis' "Now Hiring" sign would soon be prominently displayed in the door.

No one seemed to notice the other change in the scenery. At the shop next door to the construction company, the lights were out and the door was closed. A discrete, hand-written sign on the door read: "Brother's Print Shop moved to 50543 Lincoln Parkway."

The stories by Teldon and the other reporters were predictable. A few papers chose to laud Davis in their editorial pages. The tone was optimistic for real change in the impoverished areas of the city.

In the state Senate, the Fair Wage bill was passed unanimously by the Senate Labor Committee. Statehouse observers predicted quick passage by the full Senate, which would rush the bill toward becomming law.

As usual, Sam Janus was not satisfied with the media

coverage of Laughton Park. His story came out the day after the Senate committee action.

Dependence will keep
Laughton Park Poor

by Sam Janus

Washington City -- We haven't visited Laughton Park in a while, and my, how things change. The supposedly evil Mitchell Person is no longer present and has been replaced by the supposedly angelic Ron Davis. If that alone doesn't make your head spin, then take a closer look.

Person's Fine Woodworking was purchased, eventually, by Davis and renamed Laughton Park Construction. It appears this will be the minority extension of Davis Construction Company.

According to the well-rehearsed news conference this week, Davis' new company is not in the business to make money, but rather to create jobs. They don't promise to hire everyone right now, but they say that everyone who wants a job has a right to a job.

Do you see the problem with this? Shouldn't there be some requirement that the future employees make a product that someone actually wants to buy? It's nice to guarantee a high salary, but is it too much to ask that the workers give back some kind of skill?

If you think that people have a right to whatever high-paying job they want, then I invite you to my office. Reporting doesn't pay so well these days, and I've always wanted to try my hand at the much-more-lucrative field of open-heart surgery. Come on over, and I'll give your ticker a look. Of course, you'll have to pay me a fair union wage.

What's really going on here? It's a continuation of the cycle of dependence. The message from Davis and our friend Seth Howard is, "Hey you Blacks. Your skills are so worthless that you can't get a job unless we are willing to lose money giving you one. In fact, we don't even care if you give us anything in return, other than your votes come next election. Aren't we nice?"

There is no encouragement in their actions. There is nothing to help underprivileged men and women see their own self-worth. In fact, they are only helping people sink further in despair. Is anyone really happy with money they didn't earn?

Under the infamous Person regime, the workers had a true love for their craft. That is what brought them together and made them successful. Let's see what the new regime brings.

By the way, we were looking closely at the photo that accompanied the *Times-Union* story on Davis' news conference. We've reprinted it in this paper, along with an enlargement of one section of the photo. Take a look at the sign on the door. Unless our eyes are playing tricks on us, it appears the construction company's nearest neighbor has moved to a new location. Must not have been too enthused about living in a nirvana created by Davis.

TWENTY-FIVE

"I tell ya Seth, this Laughton Park company is a goddamn mess. We hired a bunch of Blacks to make us look good, but it's almost like we picked the worst ones. The sons-a-bitches just don't show up. The machines have been breaking down. No one is taking care of anything, and the building is starting to look shitty." Ron Davis was in the lawmakers office. They were celebrating the passage of the Fair Wage bill. They were enjoying a drink before going to the governor's office for the ceremony to sign the bill into law.

"Yeah, but you're putting some life back in that neighborhood. Those people have some hope and a few of them even have jobs. Doesn't that make you feel good?" Howard asked.

"I'd feel a whole lot better if they seemed to appreciate it. Jesus, don't they have any pride in their work? I mean, we're getting some contracts, and they're getting the job done, but it's not very good. I guess I shouldn't care as long as the clients pay."

"You losing much money there?"

"Criminy. You better believe it. They aren't productive enough to cover their own payroll. I'm subsidizing it through my regular company though. One of the good things is that they are paying dues, so some of the money I'm dumping into their salaries eventually comes back, but I don't know how long I want to let this hemorrhage bleed."

"You've got to stick with it at least a couple of years, otherwise you'll look like a quitter," Howard said as he refilled their glasses.

"Don't worry, I can keep it afloat for a few years if it doesn't get much worse. Another good thing about this is my image. That PR prick I got knows his stuff. There are companies standing in line to hire either the new business or my old one, just so they can show the world they care. They are dying to appear selfless."

"It didn't hurt you to have the reporters covering that first day of applications when the line went around the block, and then following up as the lucky ones reported to work." Howard then laughed, "I must admit I was a little jealous of all your coverage, but it helped our bill."

Davis took a long sip. "The only thing I worry about is that the clients will notice poor work and my credibility will be hurt in the long run."

"Person found some good workers in that neighborhood. And I know his people all left, but couldn't you find anybody with some experience."

"Oh, we hired experienced guys right off the bat. Some of them were pretty good workers too. Problem was, the shitty guys were goofing off so much that the good workers were carrying the load. They were working twice as hard, but getting the same salary as the jack-offs. I was going to promote some of them to give them more responsibility and more money, but I owed promotions to some guys from Davis Construction, so I moved them over to the Laughton Park company. The hard-working Blacks got fed up and left."

They finished their drinks and got up to put on their suit coats. Howard had another question. "But you've always had disparities between the strong workers and weak ones. Why can't you handle it this time?"

"I don't know exactly. I think we might have played up the right-to-a-job angle too much. These guys look like they believe that this job really is their constitutional right. They have no intention of earning anything. They don't think they have to."

Davis thought about it some more, then added, "My union has always stressed that if a man works for a company, then the company can't just get rid of him. I believe the man does have a right to that job whether his production slips or not. And quite frankly, we've carried some people just to keep the dues coming in. But there's always been a loyalty to the union. In fact, the people who slip the most are some of our strongest members.

"In this new place it's different. The guys come in and expect us to protect them no matter what. They keep paying dues, but I wouldn't call them loyal. It's like they believe they are owed this job whether the union is there or not. And really, it's not like they feel they are owed the job, just the paycheck. They have no more attachment to construction that they do sweeping streets or flipping burgers.

"I wish those good guys had stuck around. I think they could have showed these jokers how to earn a living. They don't listen to the supervisors I got in there. Probably shouldn't have sent in white guys to run things."

"I wonder what happened to Mitch Person," Howard redirected the conversation. "Why don't you track him down? We haven't heard anything from him since he sold out."

Davis got that twinge in his gut that came every time he thought about his daughter and Person. Truth be known, he too was curious about the activities of Mitchell Person, if for no other reason than to find out for certain if he was the broken man Davis assumed he was. That Person sold his own business caught both Davis and Howard off guard. They really didn't think he would give up that completely. Davis had looked forward to a long, agonizing victory over Person. The fact that he just sold out and vanished made Davis feel like something was left unfinished.

Several times he thought about sending his PI out to check on Person, but as far as he knew, Sandy was still dating the guy. He couldn't bear the thought of the slimy detective taking pictures of his daughter in a compromising position.

He answered Howard quietly, "I'd rather let him rest in peace."

They continued their walk to the governor's office.

Davis added, "The other thing that pisses me off is that those other companies skipped out on me. I was at least counting on some rent money to keep the construction company going, but those other businesses just up and moved out. Now I've got a shitty business and a couple good-for-nothing empty buildings."

At the governor's office, the men met with Rev. Walker and the governor. The media gathered to capture the signing ceremony and catch the prepared comments from each of the men present. Another story about Laughton Park and Fair Wages put to bed, most of the reporters were glad it was finally over. They were tired of the posturing and the rhetoric.

TWENTY-SIX

Remember Laughton Park?

by Sam Janus

It's been several months since the definitely white Ron Davis and the definitely white Seth Howard took over the Laughton Park enterprise zone to help the definitely Black residents of that area.

You'll remember that they moved in to free the local employees from business owner Mitchell Person who had the audacity to pay them below union scale. Davis launched his new business with much fanfare, promising to pay union wages and hire nearly everyone who thought they had a right to a job.

The *Endurance* decided to visit Laughton Park and see how things are going. Guess what. They suck.

Ron Davis' experiment with a business devoted entirely to the needs of the worker over the needs of the business is biting him on the ass. The place looks awful.

The fine renovation that Person made before he left has been ruined. The other Laughton Park businesses moved out. And last month, some clod dropped a lit cigarette in a pile of sawdust and set the place on fire.

The fire was put out, but we're guessing Davis wishes it had burned down. Our sources tell us his Laughton Park Construction company is losing big money. Apparently, the work quality is so bad that repeat customers are nonexistent and word-of-mouth is steering business away.

But he can't close it, can he? How can the big union boss close the very business that embodies the rights of workers?

This situation calls for the kind of insightful analysis that you've come to expect from the *Endurance*:

The problem in Laughton Park is not with the race of the workers. Davis hired workers from the same neighborhood that Person hired from when he was running the place. But Person's business was thriving. Even during the protests, Person was winning bids for construction projects.

It's the same type of business, in the same building, with workers from the same neighborhood. So why is Davis' company flat.? The difference is that Person's company relied on unsurpassed quality to stay in business. Davis' company relies on sympathy for workers, particularly African-American workers, to stay in business.

It comes down to selfishness, but be careful on how you view it.

Selfishness may not be the evil that we have been taught since childhood. Perhaps selfishness is the driving force that has been responsible for the advancement of our society, both economically and socially. No doubt selfishness was the driving force behind the workers at Person's shop.

They were completely devoted to achievement. Not achievement according to your definition or mine, but achievement according to their own standard higher than anyone else could put on them. Their motivation is not based on what they accumulate, but on what they leave behind.

Ron Davis and his crew of buffoons is devoted to something else. I don't know what to call it, but it's an example of what we've been taught selfishness is. These people are after money, with no regard for earning it. They want stuff...No, they *demand* stuff. They are devoted to getting things for themselves, by hook or by crook. This is what people typically think of when you mention selfishness.

But you can't call that "selfishness." Think about it. Everything they get in their supposedly "selfish" quest depends on what has been done, created or earned by someone else.

It can't be selfishness because it depends on something other than the self. It's dependence. The more you are dependent on others, the less dedication you have to your own needs, your own spirit.

We can't leave Laughton Park without one last

question...Where is Mitch
Person these days? Where
are all those proud, skilled
craftsmen from Person's
Laughton Park? If anybody
sees them, tell them to
contact their friends at the
Endurance.

****

Davis sat in his office and fumed. He was stuck with a
lousy business in Laughton Park, and he couldn't figure out a
graceful way to get rid of it.

His problem stemmed from all the hype Laughton Park
Construction received. It was supposed to be both a workers'
paradise and an African-American's ladder out of the ghetto. But
it was only a loafers' paradise.

These new workers just would not do a good job. They
had no work ethic and no concern for the company's well-being.
There was no realization that the company had to have a decent
product going out to get money coming in.

One of his supervisors explained that the people who
were working there had been oppressed for so long that they really
believed this job was owed to them. It was some kind of payoff
for years of suffering. They had been dependent on public

assistance programs for so many years that they had lost the concept of earning. They didn't seem to see the difference between collecting a paycheck from Ron Davis and collecting an assistance check from the welfare department.

As much as Davis believed in protecting workers, he could not afford to keep paying them if he got nothing in return. For years he was able to juggle his management interests as a company owner and his labor interests as a labor leader. In fact, his powerful position in both fields enabled him to keep both ends profitable. Remarkably, this was the first time he had a major conflict between his ownership of a company and his devotion to the ACC.

He wanted more than anything to cut his losses and get the hell out of Laughton Park. But if he did that, he might raise some eyebrows at ACC headquarters. Davis still called the shots there, but he knew a few young upstarts were patiently waiting for him to slip so they could take over.

Currently, Davis was weighing his options carefully. He could not carry the Laughton Park losses much longer. If he lost the helm of the union, though, he might lose even more money, if not his entire business, in the long run. He knew what the union could do. If he lost control of the bargaining process, his own workers at Davis Construction, under the leadership of a power-hungry ACC boss, could bargain him out of business. Davis himself would not have hesitated to use such a tactic.

Reflecting on how he got into this mess, Davis felt duped. He got sucked into creating the big protests in Laughton Park to build momentum for Howard's Fair Wage bill. That bill was paying off now, but Davis wondered if the bill would have passed anyway, even without all the show-boating in the rough neighborhood.

Two months ago, Howard won re-election by his widest margin yet. His biggest issue during the campaign was the "bright, new hope for jobs in Laughton Park." That "bright, new hope" was created solely at the expense of Ron Davis.

Furthermore, Howard was subsequently elected as Speaker of the House by his colleagues. Davis wondered how many votes Howard won because he had distributed money from the House Victory Campaign Committee to selected colleagues in return for votes. A good chunk of that money, Davis figured, was ACC PAC money handed over by Davis to Howard.

Davis had not talked to Howard in the past month. As much as he had been thinking about this situation, he knew he would end up accusing the new Speaker of setting up this whole thing and using Davis to get to the speaker's podium. Then Howard would feign shock and hurt and say something like, "How can you say that after all I've done for you? All those years of legislation benefitting the ACC. And aren't you benefitting from the Fair Wage law?"

Davis wouldn't have a good response, because yes, he had benefitted from his association with Seth Howard, and the Fair Wage law was as much help as he planned. It was easy to point out many other instances where Howard's actions helped Davis greatly. This current screwing was a lot more subtle. Difficult to point it out exactly.

In addition, if Davis made an accusation against Howard, he would be through. It's never a good idea to make enemies with the most powerful man in the state legislature. Much better to be a submissive ally.

So Davis kept his mouth shut. Sooner or later, he would calm down enough to talk to Howard without blurting out insults. Eventually he would need the lawmaker for another favor, so it was best to keep on his good side.

In any case, his immediate problem was in Laughton Park. It started out as a PR prize and turned into an expensive nightmare. Ironically, because the company was created primarily as a PR event, pulling out of the company would inevitably also be a PR event, albeit a damaging one.

He wished his asshole PR secretary were still around. As much as he disliked the man, Davis had to admit the PR wizard knew what he was doing. That was probably why Seth Howard hired him to join his legislative staff. Davis hadn't replaced him yet, and now the construction boss wished he had a good media manipulator.

He was alone.

That damned Mitch Person. If only that guy hadn't come along, I wouldn't be in this boat, Davis thought. A couple of days ago, Davis was so furious with his predicament that he decided he had to get revenge on Person. He called his daughter to see if he could unobtrusively find Person's whereabouts.

Her office said she was on vacation. Once he cooled down, he felt guilty and pathetic knowing he was actually willing to use his own daughter to get what he wanted. Though he had never hesitated to use people to reach his goals, he had always drawn the line at his own family. He was ashamed at how ready he was to break that one rule.

At that point, he decided not to worry about Mitch Person. At least for now.

The latest thing bugging him was the goddamn *Endurance*. Did that guy think he could continue to insult Ron Davis and get away with it? He was being called names and laughed at, in black and white. The guy should pay dearly, thought Davis.

The last time Davis wanted to bust his ass, Seth Howard stopped him. But fuck Seth Howard! Davis wanted to get some revenge on someone, and that cocky prick at the *Endurance* was as good as anybody.

But if Davis had learned one thing from Seth Howard and the PR guy who used to work for him, it was that sometimes a subtle attack is the most successful. No sense dragging himself into this if he could find a back-door way to burn Sam Janus.

He thought about calling his PI, but then decided he didn't trust that guy either. Davis planned to take care of it himself.

Grabbing the copy of the *Endurance* out of the trash can, he headed to his car. Driving to Laughton Park he planned his speech.

When he arrived at his newest, but least profitable,

company, he forgot what he was going to say. The inside was even messier than the last time he was here. No one ever cleaned the machinery. The ACC rules left that job to the night cleaning crew that all ACC shops were required to employ. It's not that the construction workers did not have the skills to clean the machines, but they wouldn't have been allowed to clean up according to the contract. The contract, after all, protected the jobs of the dues-paying cleaning crew.

But looking about the shop, he was sure it was a moot point because he knew the men he was looking at had no interest in cleaning up. In one corner, a man was stretched out with a cap over his eyes, sleeping peacefully. In the middle of the room, three other men were playing cards. It wasn't lunch time, so he knew these guys were goofing off, plain and simple.

To make matters worse, they didn't jump up and try to pretend that they were working. They knew who he was. They had met him before, though Davis couldn't remember their names. They just kept doing what they were doing, only glancing at Davis to throw him a look of contempt.

Didn't these ungrateful slobs realize who he was? They owed their jobs to him. According to what the supervisor for this company told Davis, these men believed that he owed them their jobs, not the other way around.

He wanted so badly to scream at these men if not to pull out his personal gun and shoot them right here. Watching these men loaf around his shop with that air of self-righteousness, he nearly lost his cool.

He took a deep breath, then decided to salvage as much of his plan as possible. He began to have second thoughts, considering his plan relied on these men taking action. He doubted they could do anything. He proceeded, after vowing to himself to throw these men out on the street at his earliest opportunity.

"Men, I'm glad you're here," Davis lied. "I've been reading some pretty awful things about you in this paper." He held the *Endurance* aloft.

"This paper has printed the most racist statements I have ever seen in print. It questions your right to a job and your ability to do a job. Personally, I'm offended."

The men gave no reaction. Just looked at him.

About this time, another man came out of the back room. He looked like he had actually been doing something related to construction. He had a bit of fire in his eyes.

He walked straight to Davis and grabbed the paper, which was folded to reveal Sam Janus' article.

"Thank God," thought Davis. "He can read."

After a couple minutes, the worker turned to his lazy colleagues and said, "Brothers this is serious."

With that, the other men began to stir. Davis realized that his words were nothing to these men. They weren't going to listen to some white boss. It took a Black man to lend credence to anything Davis said.

The man turned to his boss. "Mr. Davis, we'll take care

of this. I'm gonna contact Rev. Walker. No paper can print this shit about African-American men and get away with it."

Davis left. He was somewhat relieved, though he wasn't very confident that his new army could be depended on for very much.

TWENTY-SEVEN

When Mitchell Person finished the last contract awarded to Person's Fine Woodworking, he took a couple of days off. He was preparing to enter into a new phase of his life and he wanted to reflect on what he had accomplished so far.

He drove out into the woods to look at the cabin he built for the old man. It had been the first job where he was able to devote his entire existence to a construction project. It would always be special to him.

Continuing on a chronological tour, he passed the many small offices and homes where he had performed -- yes that's the right word -- renovations. He had a cup of coffee at Miller's Tavern before heading out to look over his last stop...Benham United.

The entire tour took him four days. His final stop took up the last half of that fourth day. Quite a bit had been accomplished, and he was proud of every project.

Leaving Benham, he headed to Sandy's apartment.

When he proposed, she answered "Of course."

In their relationship, there was never anxiety over where the relationship was headed, or what the other person was thinking, or if the other person was being faithful. Their commitment to each other was logical. It made sense to each of them. Therefore, it was relaxed.

Each knew they would be married eventually. They hadn't talked about it. Each trusted that the time would come when it would happen, but they didn't wonder when that time would be.

This was the time.

They spent the night together, and in the morning Sandy called her office to tell them that she was going to use up most of her vacation time. Sandy was known to put in long hours in the office, and she hadn't taken a vacation for three years.

Therefore, she had built up quite a stack of vacation days and compensatory time, enabling her to take several months off.

Fortunately, she was not behind at work. Her special projects were completed and all that remained was her day-to-day casework that could be handled by others.

She did not explain the reasons for her vacation, but her supervisor wished her well. Truth be told, he was ready for her to take a vacation. He felt uncomfortable around her, though he didn't know exactly why. It might be slightly inconvenient for her to be gone a long time, but it might be worth it, he thought.

Without telling anyone, they left town to a nearby state

that allowed no-wait marriages. The honeymoon was spent filling the days with a tour of the country, and filling the nights with intense lovemaking.

Everywhere they went, they were encouraged with bits and pieces of evidence that good, strong, proud people lived and thrived. Unfortunately, they also saw that the majority of people were lost, soul-less and striving for confused goals.

But they were able to look straight through all the sadness to see a brilliant building design here, a masterfully crafted cabinet there, a well-planted farm here, a perfect piece of pie there. At each stop, they could find some sign that other people also believed in the wonder and power of mankind's ability to create.

They were devoted to being individuals, but that didn't mean they wanted to be alone. The lasting reminders that others like them existed added energy to their days and passion to their nights.

This morning, they lay in each others arms, peering through the thin curtains in their hotel room at the rising sun. It was the last day of their honeymoon, as Sandy's vacation days were exhausted. They would make it back to Washington City by evening.

Sandy spoke first. "You know, we've never really talked about what we're going to do next. I mean, living arrangements, things like that. If it's all the same, I'd rather not move to your apartment. It's pretty crappy, and you don't even have a sofa."

"No problem. I'm not attached to my apartment or anything in it." Of course, he wasn't talking about the beautiful desk and the two sets of bookshelves he had made himself. Sandy knew those hand-made furniture items were not "things" as much as parts of him. Therefore, they would be coming with him. When they talked about the poor condition of his apartment, they only discussed the things that were not part of him.

"On the other hand," he added, "we could move to Brookview Armes."

"Do you think it's ready yet?"

"Who knows. We've been gone a long time."

Sandy laughed. "I keep forgetting that nobody knows we're married. We'll have our hands full just dealing with the reactions of friends and family."

Person winced. "Oooh. I forgot about your family, if you can believe it. Your folks aren't going to be too happy are they?"

She stopped laughing. Surprisingly, she had forgotten about her family too. It was not her intention to marry a man based on her family's approval. Her decision about her marriage was hers and hers alone. But it was not her intention to hurt her parents' feeling either.

"My poor mom. I think she'd probably given up on me getting married. I'm sure she still hoped it would happen and that it would happen in a big way. Oh, and my dad is just going to throw a fit."

She burst out laughing. "I can't image the look on his face when I tell him I'm married to you. I know he's got a special savings account set aside to throw me a huge wedding. And now he won't have that chance. Then to make matters worse, the guy

I married is the guy that's caused him all sorts of grief."

Person was puzzled. "Why is that so funny?"

"Because he'll get over it. Assuming the initial shock doesn't kill him. The thing is, he and Mom have a lot of important friends. They always try to impress those people, so I'm sure the wedding they have always dreamed about is one to make these other people envy my folks. It has little to do with my actual happiness. It's motivated more by their continual struggle to be accepted by others. I don't know, that's just kind of funny to me."

"It's not half as funny as trying to picture your dad shopping for a Christmas present for his new son-in-law."

They started laughing and wrestling on the bed.

"The other thing is that he's probably gotten over you by now," she added. "He got his new law. He stopped you from becoming competition. He'll probably put his arm around you and say 'No hard feelings?'"

"Boy, I sure look forward to that," he said sarcastically.

"What about your folks, Mitch. How are they going to react? You know, I haven't even met them."

He reached over to grab her and snuggled closer. "They are going to be impressed that I was able to find such a beautiful and intelligent woman."

Their departure from the hotel was delayed another hour.

When they finally returned to Washington City, they dropped their luggage off at Sandy's apartment and went over to Mitch's apartment to pick up some of his belongings.

Person's answering machine was blinking to indicate that he had several messages. He pressed the button to play them back. A couple of reporters called. He'd ignore those. Three people called seeking work from him. He wrote those down to call them tomorrow. One wrong number. One prank from some kids. And a recent message from Sam Janus saying he had some interesting news that Person would want to hear right away. Person found the number in his address book and called. It was late, but he knew Janus would still be in the office.

"Mitch! Man, you know how to disappear. Nobody's heard anything from you for months. I called Travis and he hasn't seen you. I've been writing about you, but you haven't responded. Where have you been?"

"Out seeing the country. It's therapeutic. You should try it."

"Well, I hope you are in good spirits. I imagine you are, and if not, I've got some news to cheer you up."

"What's that?"

"I'm about to be protested."

"What? When? Why is that good news?"

"Well, in my last column, I revisited Laughton Park. The place quickly became a shithole after you left. I'm sure that doesn't surprise you. But anyway, I spelled it out in my usual fashion, being pretty critical of the new people working there, and now several Laughton Park African-Americans are going to protest outside my office. My paper is going to be labeled racist."

Person was a bit bewildered. "But...you're Black."

"I know that, but they must not. I don't try to make my face known to people. It allows me to stand in the background and overhear important information. I don't think many people could pick me out of a group.

"It really doesn't matter that much. They're intending to attack my words, not my face. But it should be interesting to see what happens when they see me. You want to come? It's tomorrow at 1:00."

"I think I'll read about it in the papers, but thanks for the offer. Who do you suppose is behind it?"

"I'm pretty sure it was started by Ron Davis. I was hard on him in my article. He kind of got jolted in the whole Laughton Park deal, and I think he just wants to take revenge on someone. I'm as good a target as any."

"What happened to him in the Laughton Park deal?"

Janus explained the sorry state of the Laughton Park Construction company and Davis' dilemma. He also filled Person in on the ascension of Seth Howard to the Speaker's position and guessed at some of the background politics.

"So it looks like Davis got screwed," Janus concluded. "It's kind of funny really. So, what have you been doing these past months, other than touring the country?"

"I married Ron Davis' daughter."

Janus started laughing. Then stopped. "You're not kidding are you?" he asked in amazement.

****

Janus waited for the protest with mild amusement. His papers' headquarters was a poor stage for a media event. Unlike Person's construction shop in Laughton Park, Janus' shop was not out by the sidewalk. It was behind a dry cleaning shop. So the angry mob would be forced to march up and down an alley.

Furthermore, he heard through his contacts that Rev. Walker would not be taking part in the event. Mysteriously, Walker had not been the same since his protests outside Person's old company. Nobody could put their finger on what was troubling him. They said he just seemed to lose his fire. A couple of his aides said he had taken to pacing around his office mumbling things about being used, lost directions, things like that. It was incoherent to the aides.

Without Walker, the upcoming protest would lack focus and credibility. Janus knew if he walked out to face the crowd and the media saw his race, that would pretty much cripple the protest.

African-Americans may feel perfectly comfortable protesting the actions of other African-Americans. Just because they are all the same race doesn't mean they all agree with each other. There are factions among Blacks to the same degree there are factions among whites, Asians and every other race. People are people after all.

The difference comes in how it is portrayed by the media, and to a larger extent, understood by the public. The public will react a certain way when African-Americans protest racism by whites. They understand that kind of racism and know how they feel about it. But when African-Americans accuse other African-Americans of racism, the rest of the public gets confused. They can't judge the validity of the charges, so they just write it off as infighting and ignore it.

Janus understood that this protest was not going to run him out of business. The fact that he was the same race as the protestors would jumble the message of the protest in the minds of his customers. But that would be just a further jumbling of an already un-focused message. The protests in Laughton Park were carefully orchestrated media events, set to reach a particular goal. This protest would be a pointless venting of misplaced anger.

He wished he did not have to blow his cover for such a meaningless event.

He looked out the window and saw one TV crew standing around talking to a couple of other reporters. The crowd hadn't shown up yet.

A few minutes later he heard a ruckus. Sloppy looking African-American men were standing outside his door shouting slogans and looking hostile. One of the cleaner-looking men was over talking to the reporters, giving them the story. Janus could tell by the man's gestures that he was expressing outrage. He was waving his arms and periodically pointing to the copy of the *Endurance* that had him all worked up.

Finished with the protester, the reporters walked toward his door. "This is it," he thought.

He opened the door and stepped out.

"We're looking for Sam Janus," the TV reporter said.

"That's me."

For a minute, nobody said anything. Even the protesters were quiet. Just as suddenly, the reporters started scribbling in their notebooks and the protesters started yelling, "Tom! Tom! Tom!" in reference to the infamous Harriet Beecher Stowe character.

"What's your response to charges that your paper is racist," asked a newspaper reporter, trying not to laugh.

"I think this protest is just a result of confusion on the part of these men who didn't understand what my article was about and are angry that things aren't working out in Laughton Park."

As the reporters were writing the response, one of the men in the group yelled, "He ain't no brother." The other men began yelling too and someone threw a rock that missed Janus' head by less than an inch and smashed through the window on his door.

The clean-cut protester grabbed the rock thrower and tried to calm him down, but it was too late. Other men started to pick up rocks and trash and throw them at the *Endurance* offices.

This, Janus hadn't anticipated. Knowing he was the target, he ran into his office and locked the door. He was glad his other reporters were out on assignment.

The apparent leader of the protesters was frantically trying to restore order to his angry mob. The reporters had run back behind an automobile for cover and were writing furiously. The TV camera was not missing a thing.

By now, the dry cleaner had noticed a problem and called the police. Janus could hear sirens over the sound of breaking glass.

One man had climbed through the broken front window and started smashing computers and office furniture. Another soon joined him.

Things were well out-of-hand by the time the police arrived, but they quickly took control. Surprisingly, no one was hurt, though the offices of the *Endurance* were seriously damaged.

That night, the small riot received top coverage by the one station that was there. The other stations ran the story a little later because they had no footage.

As Janus had guessed, he came out looking like a hero being victimized by poor African-Americans who overreacted to something Janus wrote. Another guess, which later turned out to be true, was that the attention would increase sales dramatically.

Although he personally benefited from the event, Janus was somewhat disturbed. He hated when one minority protested against itself or another minority. The problem was that it cheapened the arguments against racist whites. White people would see these protests and shake their heads, snickering. In their thinking, if the Blacks were so confused about racism among their own people, then maybe they are confused when they call whites racists. Such confusion helped whites deny the real problems that existed.

Janus was not hung up on racism. But he knew it existed.

His victory was hollow.

TWENTY-EIGHT

Tall glass of scotch in hand, Davis sat in his darkened study. He had just turned off the TV, so the only light came from a small desk lamp in the corner.

He was brooding.

Why was everything going wrong? It felt like the passage of the Fair Wage bill was the turnabout from things really going his way to things really going against him. He was angry because that bill was suppoed to help *him*. Seth Howard had gone his own way, as if he had used Davis for whatever he was worth and was now done with him. Davis' new business was turning out worse than he could have imagined. And now this protest he staged went south. He was no PR pro, but he could tell, based on the evening's TV coverage, the public opinion would be firmly against the Laughton Park Construction company.

The only glimmer of hope was that now he might have justification for closing the place down. On the other hand, he might be seen in an even worse light if he turned his back on them now.

He took a long drink. Things were bad. But surely he had hit bottom. Surely things couldn't get worse.

There was a knock on the study door.

He turned to see his daughter peeking through the slightly opened door. Someone was behind her, though he couldn't make out the shape.

"Dad?"

"Hi honey. Come on in. I'm just moping, but I'm suddenly happier seeing that you've come to visit."

"That's encouraging." She came into the room and turned on the light.

It took a minute for it to register with him who was with her. He had never met Mitch Person before. He only knew the man from the black and white photographs his PI had provided.

When it hit, Davis froze. The tension turned from an emotional feeling to a physical entity. Davis swore he could see an electrical fog pouring out of his own head and filling the room.

"Daddy, this is Mitchell Person, and I don't know how to tell you this other than directly, so here it is...We're married."

Davis just shook his head slowly and chuckled to himself. Apparently the demons were not done toying with him yet.

For his part, Person wasn't saying anything. Not out of fear. But what would he say? This was Ron Davis' problem to work out for himself.

"When did this happen?"

"Three months ago. We got married at one of those commercial chapels and have been traveling the country ever since."

"Your mother is going to be torn up that you didn't let her plan a wedding for you."

"I know. We already told her. She's crying in the kitchen right now."

"Why don't you try to console her, Sandy. I'd like to talk to Mr. Person alone for a few minutes." When he said it, Davis hadn't yet decided whether he was going to kill Person. As Sandy left the room, he decided he didn't have the energy.

Now that he was alone, face to face with Mitchell Person, Davis realized he misjudged the man. Not that Davis suddenly liked him. No, more the opposite. He realized he had underestimated the inner-strength of Person. Apparently, Person was not just some two-bit union buster trying to make a quick buck. He was a man whose actions were born of conviction, even though those actions were not ones Davis approved of.

At the same time he gained a little more respect for Person -- as a more worthy adversary, certainly not as a friend -- he grew more uncomfortable. Davis was a man who was good at playing mind games and carrying out negotiation strategies. He didn't like the way Person's eyes cut right through all that and stared directly at his soul.

Might as well level with him, thought Davis. "Well young man, you won."

Person's expression turned to one of genuine puzzlement.

Seeing that his opponent did not understand, Davis continued. "You won the game. You beat me. You made a profit off that business of yours, stuck me with a piece of shit, and you've just about ruined me with it. Okay. I'll sell it back to you for less than I bought it. That ought to make you happy. Now, you don't have to bring my daughter into this. I know you can get to me. You're in control. And you can have your business back. You won. Are you happy?"

Again, Person returned a confused look. This time he spoke. "But Mr. Davis, I don't want that business back. As far as I'm concerned, it doesn't exist anymore."

"I was afraid you'd say that. It must mean you milked every possible bit of profit out of it. I guess I'm just stuck with a dog. You were probably happy to unload it. So what are you after? Revenge? Control?"

"Revenge and control would be a waste of my time. Why would I bother with them? Believe me Mr. Davis, and I don't mean to be insulting, but you haven't concerned me one bit. I strive to build, to create, to use my God-given skills to make physical testimonies to the wondrous powers of mankind."

Now it was Davis' turn to look confused.

Person continued. "When I'm involved in construction or renovation, I enjoy working with other men and women who have the same goal as me. I use lumber that was carefully crafted by a conscientious mill. I use tools that were lovingly created by people who hope those tools will be used for the betterment of our species. I share duties with other craftsmen who want nothing but to put their entire being into the project we are creating. I work for men and women who may not have the woodworking skills themselves, but still want to be a part of a new creation. Together, we add another level to the ever-growing pedestal on which mankind stands. It's a selfish devotion to making part of that platform that drives me.

"Revenge? Power? Control? Greed? Those are not tools for building. Those are weapons of destruction to keep other people from reaching the top of the pedestal. The men and women who don't want to climb, or are afraid they may not be able to make it, try to tear away at the pedestal. They believe they can either keep the top within their reach, or they can simulate being on top by keeping everyone else beneath them. In reality, all they do is waste time and energy that could be spent adding to the heighth, quality and dignity of the pedestal.

"You see, you can't fight the destiny of mankind. No matter how many obstacles are placed in the way of the climb, no matter how well the weapons are used, some men and women will find their way to the top.

"You and the legislature and Rev. Walker put an obstacle in front of my company. So my company stopped its ascent, but I hope you didn't think that would stop the individuals who made up that company. We are still marching on."

Davis' mouth was dry. He didn't understand exactly what Person was saying, but he thought he caught the gist of it and it wasn't particularly flattering. The bottom line was that he was still stuck with the Laughton Park business. He got up to refill his glass, not offering anything to his new son-in-law.

"What I can't figure out is why that business fell apart. I hired from the same neighborhood as you. We are undertaking the same size of projects. What's the difference?" Davis asked, mostly to himself.

Person answered anyway. "Why did you buy it? I started working there because I wanted to offer the best construction services possible and I wanted to make a profit doing it. I don't know what your real motivations were, but judging from your media statements, you created the business to create jobs for needy people. The media might buy that as a noble goal and much of the public might think you're being kind, but I don't. Just because someone is needy doesn't mean they're stupid. If their job is created without profit being the reason, they know it's just a sham. How hard do they have to work to meet the requirements of a sham? Better yet, why would they want to work hard if they were not asked to create part of mankind's pedestal? The only purpose of their work is to prove that you and Seth Howard and Rev. Walker are nice men. Where is the glory in that?"

"Listen buddy, you're getting pretty brave insulting me in my own house." Davis was getting drunk. His sharp negotiating skills were dulled considerably, so his most accessible response was anger. He hated hearing what this man was telling him. At the same time, he wanted to hear more.

But an insult is an insult, so he hollered a little louder. "Look at this house. Look at Davis Construction. Look at my cars. I am more successful than you can hope to be. How can you say I am anywhere but at the top of your so-called pedestal?"

Person shrugged. Perhaps he should have just shut up, but he couldn't. He decided he might as well make his case and let Davis sort it out himself.

"I can't deny you've acquired many things. Laughton Park aside, you've apparently found *a* way to make a profit. But how did you do it? Did you find *the* way to make a profit? Davis Construction and the ACC are responsible for most of the standing construction and renovation projects in this city if not the entire state. But how do you truly feel about those projects? Do you ever go into one of your jobs sites, years after completion, and just feel everything? Do you get the sense for how your work fits into the lives of the people who use your creation for work or for home? Has your work made their lives better and easier? And most importantly of all, when you walk away from your projects, do you feel proud?

"Your possessions are nice. But some day, you will be gone and those possessions will belong to someone else. We are only immortal through what we have created. What is your immortal contribution to mankind Mr. Davis?"

Calmly, Davis walked over to his desk and opened the top drawer. His pistol was lying there, loaded, ready to put an end to the cocky bastard who married his dau... He paused. Not that he was on the best of terms with his daughter, but killing her new husband would certainly make their relationship rocky, to say the least. In all this discussion, he had forgotten about her. With some regret, he left the gun in its place, closed the drawer and faced Person.

"Where does my daughter come into this?"

Person could not see what was in that drawer that Ron Davis just opened and closed. He had a guess, but chose not to think about it. "She is my wife, and I can't tell you how proud that makes me. Not because of her prestigious name. To tell you the truth, I didn't know you were related until we had been dating for awhile. My attraction to her is based on her spirit. She and I think alike."

Davis rubbed his face and thought about that. This was a problem that required patience to solve, if it could be solved at all.

"I have to admit it bothers me a great deal that my daughter would marry a competitor. That is, I assume you are still going to be in the construction trade and that you will continue to be non-union."

"You shouldn't worry about it. I don't think our customers are looking for the same thing. Besides, I've decided to stay small-time. As long as I am an independent contractor with few, if any, employees, I can have unlimited freedom. But the larger I grow, the more people want to obstruct me. Sure I could accomplish more if a big company of people like me could work together, but there are too many disincentives for that to be enjoyable. That's the closest I will come to letting other people control my destiny. It doesn't bother me, because I can be as happy working by myself as owning a large company. The real loser is society."

"Out of respect for the daughter that I love deeply, even though I don't understand her, I won't crush you right here. But I'll be watching. Don't give me a reason to change my mind. You see, I also am selfish. I want my business to succeed so I can continue to bring in lots of money. You aren't a threat to me right now, but I will not let you cut into my profits even one penny." Davis turned his back to Person.

Person shrugged. He wanted to explain the difference between "selfishness" which drives one to create and "greed" which drives one to hoard. But he realized he had probably pushed his luck once too often this evening. He reached into his coat pocket and pulled out a dark cigar.

"Mr. Davis," he said to his father-in-law's back, "On our trip, I stumbled upon a cigar store in the south. The old man who ran it grew his own tobacco and hand-rolled his own cigars. He did that because he knew he could make a better cigar than anyone else. He didn't sell them, because he knew they were the best, and then he would have to be making them to keep up with the demands of other people. He said that would have taken the joy out of it. I suspect his real reason was that he was tired of fighting against regulations on how many he could sell and under what conditions. Anyway, after shooting the breeze for a while, he determined I was worthy of a box of his cigars. I smoked a couple of them already. I'll tell you, he *can* do it better than anyone else."

He walked over and set the cigar on Davis' desk. "I'm

leaving one for you. I don't know why exactly. Maybe it's because you look like you could use one."

Person left Davis alone in the study. Davis' mind had stopped trying to sort out everything. Between the scotch and the multitude of emotions, his brain was shot for the time being anyway. All of the evening's events were crumpled together and shoved into a convenient in-basket in his mind to be gone through later. He just stood, numbly, staring out his study window.

Mitch wandered back to the kitchen to see Sandy and her mother sitting at the kitchen table, drinking coffee and laughing. Sandy could see from Mitch's eyes that things had been unpleasantly confrontational. She acknowledged his feelings with a glance that would let him know she understood, but without tipping her mother off to anything. The laughter continued.

"After some heavy negotiations, we've worked out a plan to save Mom's feelings," Sandy said. Her mother was laughing as she got up to pour a cup of coffee for Mitch.

"Uh, oh," said Person with a smile. The lighter mood in the kitchen lifted his spirits.

Sandy laughed. "She's agreed to recognize our wedding as the real thing if we submit to letting her throw a reception for her friends."

Person took the coffee from his mother-in-law and sat at the table. They chuckled and discussed plans for the reception and the newlyweds described their vacation.

Later, when the couple was leaving, Person noted the scent of cigar smoke coming from the study.

TWENTY-NINE

Across the river from the Laughton Park area was another blighted inner-city neighborhood. Natural boundaries, like rivers, frequently become political boundaries as well. This particular river happened to define one edge of Seth Howard's legislative district. It also marked one edge of the Laughton Park Enterprise zone.

The residents of this neighborhood, known as Brookview, were not included in many of the neighborhood revitalization projects that always seemed to be cropping up on the other side of the river.

It's not that the Brookview residents were undeserving of such projects. The residents were pretty much the same on both banks. The problem was that Brookview was out of Howard's legislative district, and the legislator who represented Brookview had made the mistake of voting against Howard's legislation a couple of times.

Any time an innovative program for inner-city neighborhoods was introduced in the legislature, Howard somehow took control of it. That was, in part, so he could take credit for it, but more cynical observers noted that it was also so he could make sure the program did not interfere with his own political philosophies. Furthermore, once he pushed it through the legislature, he would have a good deal of influence over where the program would be carried out.

Had the Brookview legislator swallowed his pride and tried to make amends with Howard, he might have gotten a couple of those programs in Brookview. But the man believed it was more important to vote his conscience, Howard be damned. Consequently, he was lucky if he could get as much as a pothole repair in his district. Remarkably, his constituents continued to re-elect him despite his inability to return many direct services to them. They respected his integrity.

One particular building in Brookview had recently undergone some changes. The Brookview Armes housing project for low income citizens had fallen in such disrepair over the years that it was no longer habitable. One resident got fed up enough and sued Washington City for the sad state of its public housing. She enlisted the help of a concerned lawyer willing to take on the case, accepting only publicity as payment.

The city lost the lawsuit, forcing it to condemn the building and build a new housing project for the residents. The city continued to own the condemned property but they were afraid to try and renovate it. They feared the bad connotations connected with Brookview Armes would cause civil rights groups to scream bloody murder at any attempts to re-open the building.

One day a young woman from the state's human services agency came into the Washington City Urban Housing office with a plan. Sandy Davis had located a couple of investors who wanted to buy the property. She told them that if they agreed to sell the property, their mayor could take the credit for encouraging private-sector investment at the same time he was securing more money to help build additional public housing. The investors were not willing to pay enough for the city to build a new building, but the city would have some money for a down payment on one, and that would beat having an abandoned building that would continue to deteriorate and tarnish the mayor's image.

Excitement flowed through the Urban Housing office. Brookview Armes was nothing but a headache for them. They were thrilled to have a way to unload it and still gain some political points for their boss. He had, after all, been angry at the negative publicity generated by the lawsuit.

The deal was cut, and the deed to the building was turned over to Sandy Davis' investors.

The investors immediately hired a young man named Willie Bender to oversee the renovation of the building. He, after all, was the one who first spotted the abandoned building and recognized its potential. Bender explained his idea to Sandy, who looked for investors.

Eventually, she found an interested Tom Benham. He was still impressed with the work that had been done on his office building, and he recognized the commercial potential of such quality work. He rounded up a few other monied people to help underwrite their scheme.

They met with Willie Bender and Sandy to discuss their plans. It was decided that they would transform Brookview Armes into a combination apartment building-office complex. They would implement a screening process to ensure that all the businesses located there would be devoted to quality. The owners and workers of those businesses would have first dibs on the living quarters.

In addition, they loaned money to the executive managers of Person's other Laughton Park businesses. This enabled those managers to get the loans that banks likely would not have granted and purchase their businesses. Because of the potential lost revenue caused by impending protests, Person and company were happy to sell the businesses to the people they had picked to run them. Consequently, the managers were able to use Benham's money to buy their companies at a lower price than the companies were worth, though Person and his friends managed to make a profit.

Benham's investors hoped to regain their money in terms of both increased value of their Brookview Armes property and the rent from the offices and apartments. Also, they were counting on the interest payments from the loans they made to the new business owners.

Bender quickly hired the men who had been laid off from Person's Fine Woodworking and put them to work on the renovation. They had some blueprints for the apartments but not the office space. Rather, as businesses were recruited to relocate to the building, each would meet with Bender to discuss plans for their office. That way, each incoming company would have an individualized office.

The first business to sign up was Brothers' Printing. Rudy Jefferson was chased out of Laughton Park by the Fair Wage bill. He was soon followed by True Colors Painting and the other shops in the Laughton Park enterprise zone.

Person, Niles, Thomas, Elders and Ramsey decided to open a new construction company in the Brookview Armes building. Rather than it be Person's company, this new venture was merely a shared office for five individuals. No one worked for anyone else, unless one of them needed to hire one of the others to help with a project. They shared the expenses of the office, the equipment in it's shop, and the utility payments. Each was immediately hired by Bender to help with the building's renovation.

They worked together, but for themselves, shaping the once-condemned trash heap of a building into a functioning center of commerce and life.

The offices were designed so that Jefferson's printing presses and the craftsmen's tools would be muffled from other offices. One could have put a library next to Brothers' Printing without machinery disturbing the readers. The apartments were even further removed from the noise on the lower floors, which were designated for business.

Bender was the first full-time resident of Brookview

Armes. Then Jefferson. Eventually, the men and women hired to help Bender with the renovation moved in, followed by Niles, Thomas, Elders and Ramsey.

Shortly after their honeymoon, Mr. and Mrs. Person moved into the top floor, into a spacious apartment overlooking the city. Given the surrounding neighborhood, the rent was still affordable.

Following the protest that damaged his offices, Sam Janus decided to move his headquarters to the Brookview Armes building. One of his presses had been damaged severely enough that Janus had to hire someone to print that most recent copy of the *Endurance*. On advice from Person, he sought a bid from Brothers' Printing. The price and quality provided by Jefferson on that one issue persuaded Janus to forget in-house printing and contract with Jefferson indefinitely.

To handle the increased business, Jefferson hired a few of the quality workers who left Davis' Laughton Park Construction in disgust.

Gradually, but with a sure direction of its own, Brookview Armes transformed into a tower of creation. The residents above and businesses below gave the building a mind and a heart.

As strong individuals from across the state were drawn to Brookview Armes and the building neared capacity, the investors looked to the surrounding buildings for expansion.

They had made a quick, though modest, profit by buying Person's Fine Woodworking from Mitchell Person and then selling it to Ron Davis. Benham had not wanted to have any dealings with Davis, but one of his fellow investors, an older man named John Bosworth, really wanted to sell it to Davis. It was almost as if the man had a vendetta against Davis. Benham didn't understand it, but thought better of asking questions. In fact, Benham hadn't known much about Bosworth before they teamed up.

With that small profit and the rent and interest payments coming in, they were able to buy more buildings and renovate them for incoming businesses. Over time, Brookview was transformed from a rancid slum into one of Washington City's most profitable business centers.

Unlike many "successful" urban development projects of the past, the Brookview rebirth did not involve chasing local residents to other areas of the city. Many grew uncomfortable with the new surroundings and moved across the river to Laughton Park, but just as many were absorbed by the excitement of production and achievement.

Over time, Benham and his fellow investors enjoyed massive returns on their original investments. The buildings they purchased had more than doubled in value, though they would not enjoy that profit unless they sold the buildings, which they had no intention of doing, given the rental income that was generated.

In the early stages of Brookview's growth, the investors tried to keep as quiet as possible. Eventually, other businessmen and various business publications caught wind of the development. All were skeptical. Benham in particular was ridiculed and laughed at in the business pages of the *Times-Union*.

Even when the profits were evident, the paper grudgingly acknowledged Benham's luck, though they would not admit the success was planned.

For Benham, Sandy, Mitch and everyone else involved, there had been no doubt. The city's recognized business experts who had predicted failure had overlooked the undying craving for excellence.

The men and women who engineered Brookview's growth knew that as long as they were dedicated to selfishly motivated creation of which each individual craftsman would be proud, Brookview could not fail.

THIRTY

While Brookview was still in its infancy, Mr. and Mrs. Person attended the lavish affair arranged my her parents. Rather than renting a reception hall, Mrs. Davis hired a decorator to turn the Davis mansion into a lovely celebration of a young marriage.

The newlyweds specifically requested that no one bring gifts, but a few magnificent presents made it through the door. On the centerpiece table, a cake created by the best-known bakery in the city sat between two ice sculptures of lovebirds.

From the corner, chamber music by a string quartet wafted through the main hall.

The Davis bar was a hub of activity, helping the local blue bloods find merriment.

Clusters of expensively dressed, older women whispered about other clusters of women as well as the latest speculation about the new couple. Many attendees figured Ron Davis was absolutely beside himself because of his daughter's choice of husband. She could have married an important man, after all.

If Davis was feeling anguished, it did not show. This troubled the cackling hens, who felt the need to whisper further.

The groups of men, pot-bellied and gray- (or thin-) haired, stood around in their expensive suits and gossiped with a fervor equal to that of their wives. Of course, they would say they were not gossiping but were discussing politics, which was true, but what is political discussion if not gossip?

Mrs. Davis scurried from group to group thanking the people for their attendance and accepting compliments on the event, cake, etc.

Ron Davis, three scotches heavier, was in a good mood. In his heart, a small twang of pain and other more confusing feelings bothered him. It was a result of his daughter's marriage. But tonight, he was strictly in the mood to celebrate.

He loved having important people at his impressive home. And his mood was lifted even further by the fact that he recently unloaded the Laughton Park Construction company.

His first step had been to resume communications with Seth Howard. That gave him access to some good advice and possible help, should he need it.

Then he closed the company, citing his "shame" over the violent protest caused by his workers. To reduce some of the backlash, he offered to sell the business to anyone who wished to take over.

Of course, no one did. But at least he could say he was willing to let the company keep operating in the needy neighborhood.

He was criticized by his former Laughton Park workers, who staged another protest outside their own shop, eventually getting out of control and trashing the place. Now it was unsellable, Davis looked like a victim, and he got to write off the loss of equipment on his taxes.

It worked out beautifully. He had to give some credit to his former PR secretary who helped him on behalf of Howard's office. But all in all, Davis was feeling pretty pleased with himself these days.

Working the crowd with graceful precision, Seth Howard shook every hand at the reception. Though he looked like he was moving at random, he was purposely planning his path so he would reach the happy couple last.

For their part, Person and Sandy were having a pretty good time. They didn't necessarily like the people in the room, but they didn't dislike them either. Therefore, they wandered about, carrying out meaningless conversations and watching with overall amusement.

They had recently moved into their Brookview Armes apartment, much to the dismay of her parents, who were not aware that it had been sold and renovated. Shortly after they got back from their honeymoon, Sandy quit her state job and began working as the full-time investment coordinator for Benham. Her knowledge of government regulations, as well as degenerated properties that might be had for a song, made her invaluable to Brookview's planned growth. Mitchell had just settled into his new shop in Brookview.

Their mood was one of contentment.

Eventually, they saw the Honorable Seth Howard approaching them. He was smiling his perfect politician's smile, but both newlyweds saw that his eyes were more intense, yet playful. He hugged Sandy and kissed her on the cheek, then shook Person's hand. He babbled some typical greetings and well-wishings to appease all the onlookers.

In a lower tone of voice he started talking to Person. "It's good to see you again, Mitch. You have been an interesting character in this game. In an odd way, I am in gratitude to you for your inadvertent help in my ascension to the Speaker's chair. Of course, you realize it is a debt I will never pay. Don't have to."

"Just as well," said Person.

Howard turned his attention to Sandy. "May I borrow your husband for a moment. I'd like to talk to him in private for a few minutes."

She eyed him suspiciously. Through her father, she had known Howard for years, long enough to realize he was never up to anything good. She looked at Mitch and shrugged.

The two men walked to an unobtrusive door as she watched. They went outside to Howard's limousine that he had rented for the gala. The chauffeur held the door for the men, then, on cue from Howard, walked about thirty feet from the car so he would not overhear any of the conversation.

Howard poured two drinks from the limo's liquor cabinet. "Fate has always fascinated me. I've been a very successful man, not because I try to control fate, but because I have always tried to put myself in a position where fate will happen around me.

"For instance, I met with you once before, not exactly sure what would happen. But when fate pointed things in the right direction, I jumped. It worked out very well for me.

"Now, I'm sitting with you again. Had I tried to control fate, I would not have bothered trying to meet with you again, but circumstances have brought us back together, so I am jumping at the chance to see what makes you tick."

Person had been participating in this "secret" meeting with little interest. He wasn't sure what Howard wanted, and he didn't really care.

"Seth, it should not be a puzzle to you. Unlike the people you associate with every day, I am what I say I am. I have no hidden agenda. I'm not trying to get anything from anyone. I am what I do, what I create. More specifically, I am the soul that drives me to create."

Howard evaluated him carefully. Person's eyes slightly unsettled the lawmaker when they first met. Usually, Howard was the one who stared right through people to inspect all the strings and levers that could be manipulated. Person was the first man who met the gaze with one of equal intensity. Furthermore, it was odd for the lawmaker to see that Person's strings and levers were right out in the open, yet they would be nearly impossible for any outsider to control.

"Yes, yes, yes. I've heard you talk about your devotion to your own selfish interests. In fact that attitude is what led to your undoing in Laughton Park. You have to know that most people are uncomfortable with those kinds of statements. They will resent you and fight you at every turn. So why do you persist? That is the thing that amazed me through the whole affair. Why did you keep walking head-first into every trap? It's like you shunned every opportunity to dig yourself out."

Person shrugged. "People who are uncomfortable with a selfish attitude are uncomfortable with themselves. Why should I change my behavior just to make them feel better? Does that help them? Are they better off being uncomfortable with themselves, yet thinking they are superior because they have some strange selfless attitude?

"It's human nature to work for the betterment of oneself. Devotion to individuality is responsible for every great leap forward for mankind. The people who try to fight selfishness are fighting their very nature. Their souls are in constant turmoil in their natural effort to please themselves and their imposed effort to please others," Person thought it over a moment, then added, "It must make their lives very confusing."

Howard smiled at him. "Such an innocent approach. I see those confused people as an opportunity. Yes, they're fighting an inner battle between what their souls want to do and what society says they should do. And guess what? *I* am society.

"It's not natural to devote oneself to others. Therefore, people need guidance to know how to do it. I get to help them make those decisions. I tell them what is fair and just and important. They are happy to hear it. They don't have to bear the burden of discovering what others need and how they can help, they merely have to listen to me. I ease their burden by telling them what to do, how to spend their money, how to act or not to act."

"But you don't tell them what other people really need," Person responded. "You set up these systems that make people dependent on you, either for help with their problems or for help with knowing how to fight their inner drive for individuality. Aren't you just misleading people? How does that help them?"

Howard took a long sip through a big smile. He set his glass down to refill it. "Mitch, I don't give a damn about helping them. This system helps *me*. I didn't create this system, but the wave of fate took me right to the top. You see, I too am working for my own self-interest. That's what drives me. So you and I are actually a lot alike."

Person was appalled. "You view the difference between us as a fine line, but I see it as a chasm so deep and wide that it is un-crossable."

He continued. "What you are after is not self-interest. You are just as dependent on those people as they are on you. How can it be in the interest of your self, your soul, to be dependent on millions of people with confused inner drives?"

"Whatever," said Howard as he took another sip.

At that moment, Person realized he had overestimated this man. Initially, he actually enjoyed talking to another man who, no matter how twisted, understood the nature of individuality. Alas, the lawmaker didn't really understand it at all.

"The other problem with your logic, Seth, is that you twist

a lot of individuals who mean well. Some groups get started to right some wrongs that are denying people an opportunity at self-actualization, but their objectives quickly sink into your swamp of power-plays."

The legislator laughed. "Don't blame me for all of it. Like I said, I inherited most of this. But you're right. And I suppose you're talking about the ACC."

"I didn't mean to make you solely responsible," chuckled Person. "I just lumped you in with the others who think like you. And yes, I was thinking about the ACC. I'm sure at one time that group was created because management was stupidly creating working conditions that stifled the potential of employees. Those employees were right to rise up and demand a chance at individuality and achievement. But then the union got caught up in its own organizational life, rather than the lives of its individual workers, and the union became the force that stifled individuality."

"Ah, this is my specialty," said Howard. "Activist groups, bureaucracies, all of those play right into my hands. I give them a sip from the fountain of power and they quickly forget what they wanted in the first place. Soon, they are concentrating on how they can get another drink. They love me."

"That power. That need to control someone else. Ugh," said Person in a disgusted tone. "I suppose some people think it's easier to get ahead by putting someone else under them than by striving to reach higher. But reaching higher, and getting there, is so much more rewarding."

Howard was reflecting in his own power and didn't notice

the insult. "By the way, Act Now is another group that sold out quickly. Many of their constituents are still denied an opportunity for individuality. But Rev. Walker gets so caught up in protests and media that he forgets what the hell he's doing. Actually, he retired about a month ago, but the new kid who is taking over is just like him."

"I'll have to admit I was a little surprised at why I was being attacked," Person said frankly.

"It's too late for you to do anything, so I don't mind admitting that you were really close to making a difference in Laughton Park. I think Walker could just as easily have been on your side. But you were a threat to my power base, consequently, his power base, so we got things turned around. Once again, fate was kind to me. You were stopped before much could happen."

Person didn't say anything. He sipped his drink and smiled to himself thinking about the new possibilities in Brookview.

Howard broke the spell. In a serious tone, he said, "Don't think for one second I don't know what's going on across the river. It may not be in my district, but that doesn't mean I don't know about it or that I can't squelch it."

A bit stricken, Person responded, "Why haven't you tried to stop it then."

Howard thought for a moment. Then said, "I tried. Unfortunately, it got going too quickly. By the time I caught on, it was promising enough that the mayor wanted to keep it alive. He's scoring some big publicity points. I agreed not to touch it, and now the mayor owes me a favor. You see, I came out ahead again."

"Why tell me all this?" Person asked.

"Ah, you won't take the time to use any of this information against me. If I tell you where to get a good bargain on boards you might get excited, but this political life doesn't really interest you."

That's right, thought Person. The two men sat quietly for a while. Person wasn't exactly sure why he had been called out to this car. Perhaps it was a cleansing session for Howard. Maybe he needed someone to talk to. Dependence dies hard.

Realizing nothing else was to be said, Person downed his drink and got out of the car. Seeing Person leave, the chauffeur came back to the car to drive home the most powerful politician in the state.

Walking back to the house, Person reached in his suit coat pocket and touched one of the cigars that he picked up on his vacation. He thought about the care that went into making the cigar. He thought about his new home in Brookview. With renewed faith in the human spirit, he took a deep breath and headed into the house to get his wife and go home.

ABOUT THE AUTHOR

Kyle Hannon's inspiration for *The Break Room* came from the six years he worked in the Indiana Statehouse. Most of that time, he worked in the field of media/public relations for one of the legislative caucuses. A one-year stint was spent as the scheduler and legislative assistant for the state Superintendent of Public Instruction. Hannon holds a bachelor's degree in Political Science from Ball State University and graduate degrees in public affairs from Indiana University. He lives in Indiana. *The Break Room* is his first novel.

If you liked *The Break Room,* then order copies for your friends.

To order, send payment with this page (or a copy) to Filibuster Press, 55836 Riverdale Drive, Elkhart, IN 46514-1112.

Order Form

Please send ___ copies of *The Break Room* to the following address:

Name _____

Street _____

City_____ State ___ Zip _____

$10.95 per book   _____
Ind. residents add 5% sales tax   _____
For shipping add $1.95 for first   _____
   book and 75¢ for each additional book
Total   _____

Please send check or money order. Do not send cash.

☐ Please keep me informed of future Filibuster Press publications.